A Vow
for Always

THE
DISCOVERY
PART 6 OF 6

A Lancaster County Saga

A Vow
for Always

WANDA &
BRUNSTETTER

BARBOUR
PUBLISHING

Print ISBN 978-1-62029-147-4

eBook Editions:
Adobe Digital Edition (.epub) 978-1-62416-419-4
Kindle and MobiPocket Edition (.prc) 978-1-62416-418-7

All scripture quotations are taken from the King James Version of the Bible.

This book is a work of fiction. Names, characters, places, and incidents are either products of the author's imagination or used fictitiously. Any similarity to actual people, organizations, and/or events is purely coincidental.

Cover design: Kirk DouPonce, DogEared Design
Cover photography: Steve Gardner, PixelWorks Studios

Published by Barbour Publishing, Inc., P.O. Box 719, Uhrichsville, Ohio 44683, www.barbourbooks.com

Our mission is to publish and distribute inspirational products offering exceptional value and biblical encouragement to the masses.

Member of the
Evangelical Christian
Publishers Association

Printed in the United States of America.

Thou hast turned for me my mourning into dancing:
thou hast put off my sackcloth,
and girded me with gladness.

PSALM 30:11

CHAPTER 1

Darby, Pennsylvania

"Is it true, Eddie? Do you really remember your name?" Susan asked excitedly as she rushed into the living room. "I just got home from my shift at the hospital, and Grandpa gave me the good news."

He looked up at her from his seat in front of the fireplace and nodded. "I'm pretty sure my name's Luke."

"Luke's a biblical name." Susan smiled as a sense of hope welled in her chest. "Do you know your last name, Luke?"

He shook his head, a look of defeat clouding his turquoise eyes. "You'd think if I could remember my first name I'd know my last name, too, but I don't. I still can't remember anything about my past." Luke groaned. "It's so frustrating."

Susan knelt on the floor beside him and

7

touched his arm. "It'll come to you, Eddie—I mean, Luke. Just give it time. Remember what the doctors have told you. Your memory could return slowly. It's been about nine months since your accident. I think it's a positive sign that you're beginning to remember."

He stared at the fire. "You really think so?"

"Of course. Seeing Grandpa's pocket watch jogged your memory. With more time, other things will pop into your mind." Susan hoped she sounded more confident than she felt, for she really wanted to offer him hope. For that matter, she needed hope, too—that Luke would remember everything about his past and that they wouldn't discover he was married.

Bird-in-Hand, Pennsylvania

Grasping a can of insect repellant, Jonah sprayed all around the buggy shop, watching as several spiders came out of nowhere.

"This should have been done a whole lot sooner," Jonah mumbled as he finished spraying. Usually they had this job done before October, but life had gotten in the way. So that morning, Dad had been bitten by a black widow spider. Besides pain and redness, Dad had developed some muscle cramping, a headache, and nausea.

A Vow for Always

At the hospital, he'd been treated with an antibiotic, given some cream for the spider bite, and kept overnight for observation. The doctor had assured them that Dad would be alright, and luckily he didn't have a severe allergic reaction. His hand would probably be sore for a few days, and he was advised not to do any work in the shop until it felt better. Now it was Jonah's turn to carry the load, but he would do it gladly, just as Dad had done when Jonah broke his ankle.

Woof! Woof! Jonah smiled as Herbie, his folks' frisky border collie, darted into the shop with a small squash in his mouth and promptly dropped it on the floor at Jonah's feet.

"That's not a ball for you to play fetch with," Jonah scolded while he washed the bug spray off his hands. "Mom's not gonna like it when she finds out you've been stealing things from her garden."

Herbie looked up at Jonah with his big brown eyes, as though waiting for him to pick up the squash and throw it. When the dog got no reaction, he leaned down on his front legs, tail wagging in the air, and pushed the squash toward Jonah with his nose.

Jonah chuckled. "You don't take no for an answer, do you, boy?"

Woof! Woof! Woof!

He picked up the squash, placed it on the workbench, and looked for Herbie's rubber ball. He found it on a shelf near the door and cleaned it, too. "Here you go, boy—fetch!" Jonah pitched the ball out the door, and Herbie tore across the yard, yipping until he snagged the ball.

Jonah quickly shut the door so he could get back to work. As he finished up the buggy he and Dad had been working on, his thoughts went to Meredith. He still couldn't believe she'd agreed to let him court her, and he couldn't wait to spend more time with her.

Ronks, Pennsylvania

"It's been nice visiting you," Meredith told her mother, "but Levi and I really should go. I want to stop by Elam and Sadie's place on the way home and let them know that Jonah and I will be courting."

"I hope it goes well," Mom said, leaning over to kiss the top of the baby's head.

"I hope so, too." Meredith gathered her belongings and carried Levi out to her buggy.

When she arrived at the Stoltzfuses' place a short time later, Elam was home, but Sadie had gone shopping.

"Do you know when she'll be home?" Meredith asked.

Elam shook his head. "You know my Sadie. She likes to shop, and if she ran into any of her friends along the way, she's probably gabbing like a magpie."

Meredith smiled, wondering if she should tell Elam her news and let him relay the message to Sadie. It might be easier. If Sadie had anything negative to say, at least Meredith wouldn't have to hear about it today.

"Why don't ya come in and have a seat?" Elam opened the door wider. "We can visit before Sadie gets back." He grinned. "It'll give me a chance to hold my *kinskinner* without Sadie hogging him the way she always does."

Meredith didn't know whether to laugh or cry. It was true; whenever Sadie had the chance to hold Levi, she was reluctant to let him go.

"I guess we could visit awhile," Meredith agreed. "Although if Sadie doesn't get here soon, I'll have to head for home and get supper started."

"You could stay and eat supper with us," Elam suggested, leading the way to the living room.

"I appreciate the offer, but I invited my friend Dorine and her family over for supper, so I'll need to go pretty soon."

"Can I hold the *boppli?*" Elam asked.

"Of course." Meredith smiled, seeing the look of joy on her father-in-law's face. She'd just handed Levi to Elam, when Sadie entered the room.

"We didn't hear you coming," Elam said, holding his grandson gently, as if he were afraid the little one might break. "Look who stopped by for a visit."

"I'm glad you're here," Meredith said, smiling at her mother-in-law. "There's something I want to tell you and Elam."

Sadie's eyes narrowed. She looked directly at Meredith. "If it's about you and Jonah courting, I already know. What I don't understand is why you kept it from us."

"I was planning to tell you. That's the reason I'm over here now."

Sadie's mouth turned down at the corners. "It's too soon for you to be courting. Luke's only been dead nine months."

"I realize that, but it's not like I've agreed to marry Jonah. We'll just be getting to know each other better."

"Courting can lead to marriage, and it often does." Sadie's voice was edged with concern. "You may not realize it, but I'm sure Jonah has marriage on his mind." When she looked over at Elam for his support, he merely shrugged. "Do you love Jonah?" Sadie questioned, turning her attention back to Meredith.

Meredith dropped her gaze to the floor. "I think I do, although not the way I did Luke."

"Humph!" Sadie tapped her foot. "Guess there's nothing I can do about that, but I don't have to like it."

Meredith felt sick at heart. She'd known the

feelings of others would have to be considered, and instinct had told her that Sadie wouldn't take the news well. But did she have to be so rude? Meredith wished everything could be like it was when Luke was alive. She wasn't the type to think only of herself. But things were different now. She had a son to consider. Would Sadie ever accept the idea of Meredith being with any other man than Luke?

Hearing the steady *clip-clop* of a horse's hooves, Meredith glanced out the kitchen window the following morning and spotted Jonah's rig pulling in. She noticed the bounce to his step as he hurried across the yard after securing his horse to the hitching rail. A cool, comfortable day such as this would put pep in anyone's step.

Autumn was in its finest glory now that October was in full swing. After the long, hot days of summer, the cooler weather was like a breath of fresh air. The smell of wood smoke wafting from chimney tops meant warmth inside from stoves being stoked, and Meredith could see her breath when she stepped outside each morning.

"*Wie geht's?*" Jonah asked when Meredith opened the door.

She smiled. "I'm fine. How are you this beautiful day?"

"I'm doin' good, but I can't say the same for my *daed*."

"What's wrong?" Meredith asked, noticing the troubled look on Jonah's face.

"He got bit by a black widow spider. Happened while we were working in the buggy shop yesterday."

Meredith gasped. "*Ach*, my! Is he okay?"

"He showed no signs of being allergic to the venom, but his hand's pretty sore, so I'll be working in the shop by myself for a couple of days." Jonah glanced back at his horse, pawing at the ground as though anxious to go. "I'd wanted to take you and Levi for a ride to look at the colorful leaves today, but there's so much work at the shop that needs to be done, I'm afraid our little outing's gonna have to wait a few days. Maybe this Sunday after church we can go—that is, if you're free."

"Sunday afternoon would work fine for us. The leaves are just peaking, and it'll give me something to look forward to." Meredith's gaze dropped to the porch.

"Is everything all right?" Jonah asked, lightly touching her arm.

She didn't want to hurt his feelings but felt he had the right to know about Sadie's reaction to the news that they would be courting.

She lifted her gaze to meet his. "I went over to see Luke's parents yesterday afternoon and told them you'd asked to court me."

"How'd it go?"

"Elam didn't say much, but Sadie thinks it's too soon for me to be seeing anyone. She reminded me that Luke hasn't been gone a year yet."

"What do you think, Meredith?" Jonah questioned. "Are you comfortable with me courting you right now, or would you rather wait a few more months?"

Meredith shook her head. "I don't want to wait. I think once Sadie sees how good you are with Levi and realizes you're not trying to take Luke's place she'll accept the idea."

Jonah's eyebrows pulled together. "Maybe I should have a talk with her—try to make her see how much I care about you and Levi and that I only want what's best for you. I'd like to assure her that even though we'll be courting, I have no intention of changing how often they can see their grandson. I would never come between them and Levi."

"I'm sure Sadie will be relieved to hear that, but I think we should give her some time. If she doesn't warm up to the idea soon, then you might try talking to her about it."

"You're right, that's probably best." Jonah grinned. "You're not only pretty but *schmaert* too."

Meredith felt her cheeks blush. "It's nice of you to say, Jonah, but I don't always feel so smart. I'm still struggling to decide whether to rent out my house. I don't like the idea of leaving my own place and moving in with my folks."

"Would you like my opinion?" he asked.

"*Jah*, please."

"If you put your place up for rent and move in with your folks, that would take a financial burden off your shoulders. Plus, it will generate some extra income for you, and you can concentrate on taking care of Levi."

"You're right," Meredith agreed, "but things are always so hectic at my folks,' and sometimes my younger siblings get on my nerves."

"Well, I wish——" Jonah's words were cut off by the sounds of a horse and buggy arriving. When he saw Alma Beechy, he turned and started down the steps. "I'd better go now, Meredith, but I'll see you and Levi on Sunday afternoon."

Meredith smiled. "I'm looking forward to it, Jonah."

Philadelphia, Pennsylvania

"What are we going to do about Eddie——I mean Luke?" Susan asked as her sister, Anne, pulled her car into the hospital parking lot.

Anne's eyebrows arched. "What do you mean?"

"Ever since he remembered his name, he's

been depressed—more so than before." Susan frowned. "I'm really worried about him."

"He'll be fine," Anne said, turning off the ignition. "Grandpa's keeping Luke busy with projects around the house, so that should help with his depression. I'm sure that remembering his name has left Luke starving to recall everything else about his life before he came to know us, and that'll happen in time."

"I can't imagine what it's like for him, struggling to grasp details that seem to be just beyond his reach." Susan sighed. "I hope Luke gets his memory back, but I'm also scared."

"Of what?" Anne asked.

"That he might be married."

Anne touched Susan's arm. "You've fallen in love with him, haven't you?"

Tears sprang to Susan's eyes as she nodded slowly. "I've tried not to, but Luke's so sweet. I feel so happy when I'm with him. I never thought there would be someone out there for me like Luke. Even though I don't know anything about his past, what I do know of him. . .well, he's everything I've ever dreamed a man could be." She sniffed. "Maybe we made a mistake inviting Luke to move into Grandma and Grandpa's house."

Anne gave Susan's shoulder a tender squeeze. "You need to stop worrying about this. When Luke's memory returns in full, you might discover that he's not only single, but rich."

Susan snickered, despite her tears, knowing that a man's wealth didn't matter to her at all. "I doubt he's rich. If he were, he wouldn't have been wearing tattered-looking clothes when he was found unconscious at the bus station all those months ago."

Darby

"You okay, Luke?" Henry asked as the two men worked on some birdhouses in the garage. "You look a little down-in-the-mouth this morning."

Luke shrugged and blew on his cold hands. "I didn't sleep very well last night. Had a weird dream about seeing people with no faces. I've had that dream a few other times, too."

Henry set his hammer aside. "I have a hunch those faces you couldn't make out might be people from your past."

"Then why can't I remember who they are?"

"I don't know, but I think if you give it more time it'll come back to you."

"That's what Susan and Anne keep saying, but I have my doubts. If I was gonna remember, don't you think it would have happened by now?"

Henry scratched his head. "That all depends."

"On what?"

A Vow for Always

"From what Susan's told me about her work, some folks in your position get their memory back in pieces, a little bit at a time."

Luke groaned. "And some never get it back at all. The doctors have warned me about that possibility."

"Maybe for some that's true, but you've remembered your first name now. I think that's a sign you'll be able to put the rest of the pieces together soon." He thumped Luke's back. "In the meantime, we have some birdhouses to build, 'cause the annual church bazaar is just a few weeks away."

Luke picked up a piece of sandpaper. Despite his frustration, he would try to focus on the job before him and not get pulled back into the black hole of sadness that seemed determined to overwhelm him. Living with Susan and Anne's grandparents had given him a sense of family— of belonging somewhere and doing something meaningful. Even so, he longed to know if he had a family of his own. If so, where did they live? Were they looking for him, or had they forgotten he'd ever existed?

ℭHAPTER 2

Bird-in-Hand

𝒜s Meredith guided her horse and buggy down the road toward Elam and Sadie's house, a chill raced down her back. She was plagued with doubts. It had been two weeks since she'd told her in-laws about letting Jonah court her. In those two weeks, she'd only seen them at church, so she hadn't been able to speak to them privately. Meredith loved Sadie and Elam and wanted their approval.

Well, at least Mom and Dad don't object to me being courted by Jonah. Meredith glanced at Levi, asleep in his carrier on the seat beside her. *It's nice to have someone's support.*

Meredith thought about how Mom and Dad had objected when her sister Laurie had first decided to marry Kevin, who was a Mennonite. It wasn't merely the fact that Laurie wouldn't be joining the Amish faith that bothered them. It was the idea of her moving away and becoming a missionary. The Kings were a close-knit family, and it would be hard to see Laurie go.

But things didn't always turn out the way a person wanted. Losing Luke had been one of the hardest things Meredith had ever dealt with. Yet as Grandma Smucker had reminded her several times, life didn't stop because a loved one died. Meredith had made up her mind to make the best of her situation and keep her focus on raising Levi.

Meredith's thoughts came to a halt when Elam and Sadie's house came into view. She hoped they were home and would be willing to watch Levi for a few hours.

Hearing a horse and buggy come into the yard, Sadie set aside her mending and went to the door. Meredith was hitching the horse to the rail, and when she reached into the buggy and brought Levi out, Sadie smiled in anticipation.

She added a piece of wood to the slow-dying embers in the woodstove before grabbing a shawl and going out to greet her daughter-in-law and grandson.

"It's good to see you," Sadie said when Meredith joined her on the porch. "It's been awhile since we visited." She reached out and stroked the top of Levi's head. "He's growing so much."

Meredith smiled. "I know. He's doing all sorts of new things."

"Like what?" Sadie asked, motioning for Meredith to come inside.

Meredith took a seat on the sofa and pulled Levi's blanket aside. "Well, let's see. . . He's kicking and pushing with his feet; grabs for anything within his reach; smiles, laughs, gurgles, and coos. Oh, and he's sleeping through the night now."

"I'm sure that's a relief," Sadie said, taking a seat in the rocking chair across from Meredith.

"Jah. I'm finally getting caught up on my rest." Meredith smiled. "Of course, taking care of Levi and trying to get some sewing done keeps me busy. Not to mention all of the household chores that need attention."

"Is your sister Laurie still coming over to help you?" Sadie questioned.

Meredith shook her head. "She's busy getting ready for her wedding."

"What about Alma Beechy?"

"She's not helping me now, either," Meredith said. "But I'm managing to keep up with things inside, and between Jonah and my daed, the outside chores are getting done."

Sadie's forehead wrinkled. "You ought to call

on Elam more, instead of asking Jonah. I'm sure he's got lots to do at the buggy shop."

"Speaking of Elam, where is he right now?" Meredith asked.

"He had a dental appointment this morning. When he's done there, he has some errands to run."

"Oh, I see." Meredith sat quietly for a moment. Then she looked at Sadie and said, "I was wondering if you'd be willing to watch Levi while I run a few errands and take care of some business this morning."

Surprised by the offer, Sadie nodded agreeably. "I'd be happy to do that. By the time you get back, Elam might be here, and we can all have lunch together."

"That'd be nice." Meredith handed Levi to Sadie; then she reached into his diaper bag and took out a bottle. "I just fed him before we left home, but if he gets hungry before I return, you can feed him this bottle I've filled with breast milk."

"I can certainly do that." Sadie looked forward to the time she'd have with her grandson. "You can put it in the refrigerator for now, and I'll heat it up if he gets fussy."

"*Danki*," Meredith said as she started for the kitchen. "I shouldn't be gone more than a few hours."

"Are you sure you don't mind me taking today off?" Jonah asked as he and Dad mucked out the horse stalls. It had been two weeks since Dad had been bitten by the black widow, and he'd been back working in the buggy shop for the last week.

" 'Course I don't mind. We agreed some time ago that Mondays would be your day off, so if you've made plans for the day, just do 'em."

Jonah smiled. He'd been courting Meredith, and even though they'd gone for a couple of buggy rides and done a few other things together, he didn't see nearly as much of her as he'd like. Today, however, before he went to see Meredith, Jonah wanted to pay a call on Sadie and Elam, hoping he might win them over. He planned to do that as soon as he finished up in the barn.

"Anything new on that house you wanted to buy?" Dad asked, pulling Jonah's thoughts aside.

Jonah shook his head. "I made an offer on the place, but they won't come down to a fair asking price, so I decided to give up on it and look for another home."

"That's probably for the best," Dad said. "It wouldn't be good for you to overextend yourself."

"I'll just keep looking, and when the time is right, I'm sure the house I want will be there."

A Vow for Always

"Wa-a-a! Wa-a-a!"

Sadie paced the floor, patting Levi's back, trying to get him to burp. She'd fed him awhile ago, but he still hadn't burped. All he'd done was scream. She was beginning to wish Meredith hadn't left Levi with her today. It had been some time since she'd had a baby to take care of, so maybe she wasn't up to the challenge.

Sadie continued to pace, while patting Levi's back. "Come on, little fellow, give me a burp."

"Wa-a-a! Wa-a-a! Wa-a-a!" Levi cried even harder, setting Sadie's teeth on edge, until she thought she might scream herself. *I wonder if a walk around the yard might do us both some good.* Sadie went to get her shawl before she wrapped Levi in his blanket.

A knock came from the front door.

Draping her shawl over the back of the chair and keeping a tight grip on the screaming baby, Sadie opened the door. Jonah Miller stood on the porch with his straw hat in his hand.

"I'd like to speak with you," Jonah said.

Sadie frowned. "This isn't a good time. I'm babysitting Levi, and as I'm sure you can tell, he's fussy right now."

"What seems to be the problem?" Jonah asked.

Walking out to the porch, where the air was nice and crisp, and wrapping the blanket tighter around her restless grandson, Sadie hoped the change might help calm him down. "I fed him awhile ago, and he's been crying ever since," she explained.

"Maybe he needs to burp."

"Of course he does. For the last twenty minutes I've been trying to get him to do that," Sadie said with a huff as she continued to pat Levi's back.

"Babies don't always need to be patted in order for them to burp," Jonah said. "They need to be relaxed."

Sadie ground her teeth together. Who did Jonah think he was, trying to tell her how to burp the baby?

"Want me to try?" he asked, plunking his hat back on his head and extending his arms.

She shook her head.

"My twin sister has little ones, so I've had some experience burping *bopplin*."

"And I've raised my own *kinner*, so I've had more experience than you," Sadie answered, feeling more than a little miffed.

"I'd like to try."

Seeing the determined set of Jonah's jaw, Sadie finally nodded. Maybe once he saw that he couldn't get Levi to burp or stop crying, he'd give up and leave. She opened the screen door and led the way to the living room then handed Jonah the baby.

Jonah took a seat in the rocker and used one hand to hold Levi so that his backside was supported, almost like a seat. He held the little guy's head with the other hand, tipped him slightly forward, and gently lifted him up and down in a slow bounce.

A few seconds later, Levi stopped crying and let out a loud burp!

Jonah looked over at Sadie and grinned. "Works nearly every time."

Sadie couldn't believe how easily Jonah had done what she couldn't do with all her patting of the baby's back. She was also amazed at how relaxed Jonah seemed to be holding the baby as he gently rocked him. He obviously did have some experience with babies. She forced a smile and said, "Danki for getting him calmed down."

"You're welcome." Jonah cleared his throat. "Is Meredith here?"

Sadie shook her head. "She had some errands to run, so she left Levi with me. Elam's not here either," she quickly added.

"I'd like to talk to you about something," he said, stroking the top of Levi's blond head.

"What's that?"

"It's about me and Meredith."

Sadie grunted. "I know the two of you are courting, if that's what you came to say."

"That's right, and we'd like your and Elam's blessing."

Sadie stared at the floor, unable to form any words. She had a hunch from the way Jonah handled the baby that he'd make a good father. From the things Meredith had told her, she knew Jonah was kind and helpful, but could she accept it if he and Meredith got married?

"I'm very fond of Meredith," Jonah said. "And this little fellow, too." He put Levi over his shoulder and gently patted his back. "But I want you to know that I'm not trying to take your son's place. I know Luke will always hold a spot in Meredith's heart that I'll probably never be able to fill, but I will always be good to her and the boppli."

Tears welled in Sadie's eyes. "Are you hoping to marry Meredith?"

Jonah gave a nod. "When the time is right; if she'll have me, that is."

"Will you stay here in Lancaster County or move back to Ohio?"

"I have no plans of living anywhere but here," Jonah answered. "My folks are here, and I'm happy working for my daed in the buggy shop."

"If you married Meredith, would we still be able to see Levi?" she dared to ask.

"Of course. I'd want him to spend time with all of his grandparents."

Sadie sighed as a sense of relief flooded over

her. "You have my blessing to court Meredith, and I'm sure Elam feels the same way."

Darby

"It won't be long and we'll be done with this project," Henry said as he and Luke sat at the picnic table, putting the finishing touches on the birdhouses they'd been making for the church bazaar.

"It's been fun working on them," Luke said, adding a bit more red paint to the birdhouse he'd made to look like an old barn.

Henry smiled. "You've done a great job with that. If I were to hazard a guess, I'd say you've done some carpentry work in the past."

Luke's jaw clenched as he tried to recall what he had done in the past. Nothing came to mind. Nothing at all. Then a thought popped unexpectedly into his head. "Someone told me once that whenever we do anything, we should make sure we do it well."

Henry set his paintbrush aside and looked at Luke with a curious expression. "Who told you that, son?"

Luke shrugged. "I don't know. Just remember hearing it from someone before."

Henry clasped Luke's shoulder and gave it a

squeeze. "See now, Luke, you've just remembered one more thing from your past. That's a real good sign."

Luke started painting again. He longed for Henry to be right but didn't want to get his hopes up, only to be disappointed in the end.

"Look over there," Henry said, pointing across the yard.

Luke followed Henry's gaze and spotted a lazy possum ambling out from behind the woodshed and waddling away. "It's fun to watch nature," he said as a cardinal flew out of the maple tree and landed on one of the birdbaths.

"I agree. Norma and I both enjoy watching the birds in our yard, any season of the year." Henry pointed to the birdbath. "That one I keep heated during the winter months so the birds have fresh water to drink. You'd be surprised how many birds flock to that heated birdbath." He chuckled. "On really cold days, the steam comes up from the water and makes it look like a hot tub."

Luke laughed, too. He could almost picture the birds sitting around the birdbath as the steam lifted into the air. It made him think about the hot tub he'd used during therapy at the hospital and how good it had felt on his sore muscles. "Do the birds actually get in the warm water during the winter?" he questioned.

Henry shook his head. "Not to my knowledge, but they do sit on the rim and drink. Guess you could say Norma and I like to spoil our feathered friends."

"That's nice. Staying connected to nature is what sometimes kept me going while I was in the hospital. That, and the support of your granddaughters, of course."

"They're wonderful girls." Henry grinned. "Guess it's better to say, young women, since they aren't really girls anymore. But then to me and Norma, Susan and Anne will always be our special girls."

Luke was tempted to tell Henry how fond he was of his granddaughters—especially Susan. Just then the back door opened, and Norma stepped out, interrupting their conversation.

"I brought a few nibblies to tide you over until lunch," she said, placing a tray of fruit and vegetables on the picnic table.

"They look good." Henry smiled at his wife.

"There's also a small bowl of vegetable dip, if you want to pep it up a little," Norma said, taking a seat beside the men. "Oh, and I brought a jug of warm apple cider, too."

Henry smacked his lips. "There's nothin' like hot apple cider on a chilly fall day."

Norma pulled her jacket a little tighter around her neck. "It probably won't be long before we see some snow flurries." She smiled at Luke. "I really get into the Christmas spirit when there's snow on the ground."

"Maybe it'll snow on Thanksgiving, like it did last year," Henry chimed in. "But then I guess we shouldn't get ahead of ourselves. Let's just enjoy the beautiful autumn colors 'cause they won't be here much longer."

"Henry's right," Norma put in. "When the fall foliage starts in early October and lasts until early November, there doesn't seem to be enough time to enjoy the magnificent shades of autumn. Right now the mountains and valleys throughout Pennsylvania are ablaze with the most vibrant colors. Many folks like us feel there is no other season of the year more breathtaking than this one."

Luke popped a piece of cucumber in his mouth and thought about the upcoming holiday season. He wished he could remember having celebrated it before. Even more than that, he wished he knew who he'd celebrated the holidays with.

CHAPTER 3

Darby

"I've never seen so much food all in one place," Luke said as he took a seat at the Baileys' Thanksgiving table. "Least, I don't think I have."

Henry chuckled. "That's what Thanksgiving is all about—good food, and sharing it with friends and family."

"And remembering to be thankful," Anne put in.

Susan bobbed her head in agreement. "That's right, and we have much to be thankful for."

Luke sat, mulling things over. Even though he didn't have his memory fully back, he had a roof over his head, clothes to wear, and four people who really cared about him. If that's all he ever had, it was enough to be thankful for.

After taking each other's hands, bowing their heads, and listening to Henry's words of devotion and praise, they all finished with a hearty, "Amen!"

Henry stood and began carving the turkey, while Norma made sure everything was on the table.

"My mouth is watering already," Susan said, reaching for the bowl of steaming mashed potatoes. She looked at Luke and giggled. "I always go for these first."

"That's right," Anne interjected with a snicker. "Don't get in the way of my sister and her mashed potatoes. As for me, I can't wait for some of Grandma's stuffing," she added as Norma passed her the corn. "Just wait till you taste it, Luke. It's so moist and good, you'll have to go back for seconds."

"Along with bread, celery, and onions, Norma always adds some diced apple and a few chopped mushrooms," Henry added. "Anne's right—it's scrumptious!"

By now, Luke's mouth was watering. Watching Susan smother her fluffy mashed potatoes in gravy, Luke was suddenly reminded that they were someone else's favorite. But who? Was it him, or someone he knew from the past?

Even though Luke wanted to follow the thought further, everyone was having such a good time, he didn't want to spoil the festive mood. *When it's supposed to happen, it'll come to me*, he decided.

Luke handed his plate to Henry, watching as

he scooped some of the stuffing out of the breast cavity.

"How about it, Luke?" Henry asked as he continued to carve the bird. "Would you like a drumstick to start with, or do you prefer some white meat first?"

"That drumstick looks pretty good. Think I'll start with that." Luke grinned, eager to taste the golden-brown skin that covered the dark meat. He could see from the smiles across the table that the Baileys were in high spirits. He enjoyed listening to everyone as they complimented Norma on the delicious meal she'd spent most of the morning preparing.

"We always eat our Thanksgiving meal promptly at noon, because Grandma is traditional when it comes to Thanksgiving, and we wouldn't want it any other way." Susan looked at Norma with appreciation in her eyes. "By eating early enough in the day, we'll have plenty of room for dessert later on." She reached over and patted her grandmother's hand. "You did it again, Grandma. You've made another Thanksgiving feast special for all of us."

"Well now, honey, you know I love doing it. And isn't the day just perfect?" Norma added, looking out the dining-room window. "I could never figure out why, but I love it when the weather's cloudy on Thanksgiving Day."

"Cloudy outside, warm and inviting inside,"

Henry said, passing Anne the bowl of cranberry sauce. "It looks a bit like snow out there, even though they aren't calling for any. It won't be long, though," he added with a wink in Susan's direction. "Maybe you'd better get out your sled and wax up the runners."

Susan laughed. "I might do that, Grandpa."

After all the food had been passed, Luke started out with the drumstick, but he was eager to taste Norma's stuffing. The sweet potatoes still bubbled in the casserole dish, next to a bowl of fresh green beans.

"Eat slowly now, because later, we'll be having some of the pumpkin and apple pies the girls made this morning," Henry said, nudging Luke's arm with his elbow.

"Dessert is the only thing Grandma will allow me and Susan to help with when Thanksgiving rolls around." Anne winked at Norma, who still had a gleam in her eyes, watching everyone enjoy their meal.

"We can't forget the ice cream, either," Susan chimed in as she reached for a second helping of mashed potatoes. "I got vanilla, and it's a new brand that's supposed to taste like homemade."

Luke felt blessed being a part of this meal. Even though he couldn't remember any of his other Thanksgivings, he knew without a doubt that he'd never forget this one.

A Vow for Always

Ronks

Luann's forehead beaded with perspiration as she scurried around the kitchen, stirring kettles, checking on the turkey roasting in the oven, and making sure everything was just right for Thanksgiving dinner. She didn't know why, but she seemed to work best under pressure. A lot was happening in the next couple of weeks. In addition to Thanksgiving, Laurie and Kevin's wedding would take place on the first Saturday of December, and there was still much to do in preparation for that.

Keeping busy helped Luann not to worry so much, and she was worried right now—worried about Laurie becoming a missionary and concerned about Meredith and her relationship with Jonah. They'd been seeing a lot of each other lately. Luann figured it was just a matter of time before Jonah asked Meredith to marry him. It wasn't that she didn't like Jonah; he seemed very nice and was kind and attentive to both Meredith and Levi. She just had this nagging feeling that wouldn't go away, and it troubled her, thinking Meredith might not be truly happy if she married Jonah.

I can't share my feelings about all of this with Meredith, Luann thought as she lifted the lid on the kettle of potatoes simmering slowly on the stove. *I need to keep my opinion to myself and trust the Lord to work everything out for His good.*

She glanced out the window, wondering when their company would arrive. At Meredith's suggestion, Luann had invited Jonah and his folks to join them for Thanksgiving. Kevin and his parents would be here, as well as Sadie and Elam, so the house would be full when they sat down for the holiday meal.

"We're just about done here now," Laurie said when Luann poked her head into the dining room and found Laurie and Meredith putting the finishing touches on the two large tables that had been set up to accommodate their family and guests.

Luann smiled. "Things are getting done in the kitchen now, too, so once our company arrives, we should be able to eat."

Meredith stepped over to Luann. "Before everyone gets here, there's something I'd like to talk to you about, Mom."

Luann's mouth went dry. *Has Jonah already proposed? Is that what Meredith wants to say?*

"Is anyone else in the kitchen?" Meredith asked.

"Not at the moment," Luann replied. "My *mamm* went to her room to change her dress; your daed and brothers are in the barn; and Kendra's keeping the younger ones occupied in the living room."

A Vow for Always

Meredith motioned to the kitchen door. "Let's go in there so we can talk."

When they entered the kitchen, both women took a seat at the table. "What'd you want to talk to me about?" Luann asked.

"I've found someone to rent my house, and I was wondering if Levi and I could move back here for a while—until things improve for me financially."

Luann took Meredith's hand and clasped her fingers. "You and Levi are welcome to stay here for as long as you like."

"Danki, Mom, I appreciate that. I know you and Dad have your hands full, but with Laurie getting married and leaving soon, I can be here to help out."

Luann breathed a sigh of relief. Since Meredith would be moving in with them, maybe she wouldn't feel the need to marry Jonah, should he ask. She and the baby would be surrounded by their family, and Luann would make sure their needs were met, even if it meant making some sacrifices. After all, that's what families were for.

When Meredith returned to the dining room, she was pleased to see that Laurie had filled the glasses with water and everything was ready.

Now all they had to do was wait until their company arrived.

"I think I'd better see how Mom is doing," Laurie said, brushing past Meredith on her way to the kitchen.

Meredith smiled. She knew her sister was getting nervous about her upcoming wedding, which was probably why she wanted to keep busy. Meredith understood that. She'd felt the same way before she and Luke were married.

Meredith moved to the window and stared out toward the barn. She could hear joyous sounds of laughter coming from the yard, where her younger brothers raced through the fallen leaves, chasing each other, as well as the dog they'd recently acquired. He'd been abandoned at the schoolyard, and the boys had brought the mutt home. Of course, Mom couldn't say no to their sad looks, so now Freckles, the brown-and-white mixed terrier, had a new home.

Meredith's thoughts went to Fritz. When she and Levi moved here, she'd have to bring the dog along. She wondered how well he'd get along with Freckles. If it turned out to be a problem, she might have to ask Luke's folks to take Fritz. That had been his home before Luke and Meredith got married, so maybe he'd be happy there.

Meredith was glad Luke's parents had been invited to join them for dinner. Since none of Luke's siblings had been able to come for

Thanksgiving, Sadie and Elam would have been alone today if Mom hadn't extended the invitation.

Meredith had been feeling a lot better about things since Sadie now accepted the idea of her being courted by Jonah. She hadn't said anything to Mom or anyone else in the family, but she had a feeling Jonah would ask her to marry him sometime in the spring. She'd begun praying about what her response should be. She cared deeply for Jonah and was sure he would be a good father to Levi. But did she love Jonah enough to be the kind of wife he deserved?

Pushing her thoughts aside, Meredith noticed the low-hanging clouds that threatened to unleash the drizzle that had been predicted for Lancaster County. That was okay with her. She was never disappointed when Thanksgiving Day was overcast or even snowy. It was sort of a prelude to the Christmas season.

Continuing to stare out the window, as her breath steamed the glass, Meredith looked beyond the yard into the fields, catching sight of the baled hay that was ready to be brought into the barn.

Suddenly, an image of Luke came to mind, and she was reminded of last Thanksgiving, when they'd had the meal at their house. They'd invited both of their families to join them for the feast, and everyone had been in good spirits throughout the day. Even though Meredith had been a bit frazzled getting everything ready that morning, the meal and all the trimmings she'd prepared had turned out quite well.

Meredith rested her forehead against the cool window glass and sighed. When she'd first learned that Luke had been killed, she'd felt guilty for all the times they'd disagreed on things and thought she could never be happy again. Now, just ten months later, she felt a sense of peace, and a reason to go on living. Not only had God blessed her with a precious son, but now she had Jonah and his friendship.

Soon everyone would be sitting around the tables. It would be wonderful to enjoy Thanksgiving with those who meant so much to her.

My son is blessed, even though he doesn't know it yet, she thought. *If things work out between me and Jonah, Levi might end up having three sets of loving grandparents instead of the normal two. Well, I shouldn't let my thinking get carried away; Jonah hasn't asked me to marry him yet.*

Meredith headed back to the kitchen to help with any last-minute tasks. One thing she wanted to make sure was that when all the family sat down to dinner, the bowl of mashed potatoes would be sitting right next to her plate. Everyone knew Meredith got first dibs on her favorite part of the Thanksgiving feast.

CHAPTER 4

Bird-in-Hand

Where's Dad?" Jonah asked when he stepped into the living room and found his mother on the sofa by herself. "We need to leave now if we're gonna be on time for Laurie and Kevin's wedding."

"He went out to the buggy shop. Said he wanted to check on something before we left," she replied.

Jonah grunted. "He picked a fine time to be doing that. We should be on the road already."

Mom flapped her hand. "Ach, Jonah, just relax. You'd think you were the one getting married today."

Wish I were, Jonah thought. *I'd give nearly anything to be marrying Meredith today. I just need to be patient and wait till the time is right.*

"Think I'll go out and see what's taking Dad so long," he said.

Mom rolled her eyes. "Go ahead if you must, but I think you're being too impatient."

As Jonah headed out the back door, he heard Herbie barking. Then he caught sight of the dog running out of the buggy shop, yipping like his tail was on fire.

"What's the matter, boy?" Jonah asked when Herbie dashed up to him and started pawing at his pant leg.

Woof! Woof! The dog raced back to the buggy shop, as though he was trying to coax Jonah to follow.

Sensing that something was amiss, Jonah quickened his steps. When he stepped into the buggy shop, he found Dad trapped between a buggy and the floor.

"Dad!" Jonah hollered, rushing across the room. "What happened? Are you hurt?"

"Th–the buggy. . .slipped off the prop. . .and has me pinned," Dad panted in raspy breaths. "It's. . .tight against my. . .chest and hard. . .to breathe."

"Stay calm, Dad; I'll get you out of there," Jonah said, trying to compose himself.

Using strength he didn't know he had, he lifted the buggy off Dad and put its frame back on the prop where it had been.

Dad stood, but after a few seconds, he started to fall. Jonah was able to catch him and help him lie on the floor. "It's okay, Dad; I've got you."

A Vow for Always

Dad's breathing improved, and the color started coming back to his face. "Just stay put," Jonah instructed. "I'm going to the phone shack to call 911."

Just then, Jonah's mother rushed into the shop. "What happened?" she asked, with a look of alarm.

"Go to Dad!" Jonah pointed to the spot where Dad lay on the floor. "He got pinned under the buggy, but he's breathing somewhat better now. Stay with him while I go and call for help."

Paradise, Pennsylvania

Meredith smiled as she watched Laurie and Kevin take their places at the front of the Mennonite church, in readiness to say their vows. Joy radiated from both their faces, and Laurie looked lovely, wearing a modest, beautiful, white satin dress. Kevin, dressed in a dark suit and white shirt, looked equally handsome.

As the young couple looked lovingly into each other's eyes, Meredith's thoughts went to Luke. It was hard to believe he'd been gone nearly a year. So much had happened since then—Levi's birth, putting their house up for rent, and now being courted by Jonah, a man Luke had never met. But over the last couple of days, Meredith had sensed that if Luke had known Jonah, he would have had a good opinion of him, just like everyone else in their community did.

Continuing to watch her sister's wedding, it was hard for Meredith not to think about the day she'd wed Luke. Other than the birth of her son, her wedding had been the happiest day of her life. She and Luke had been joyous, filled with dreams for the future.

Things had changed the day Luke left for Indiana. No one planned for disaster. Without warning, tragedy had ripped her heart out. But as much as she hadn't wanted it to happen, life had moved forward one step at a time.

Meredith glanced around the church. *I wonder where Jonah is.* He and his folks had been invited to the wedding, and they'd said they would be here. It seemed strange that they hadn't come. It made Meredith wonder if everything was okay. Surely they hadn't forgotten.

She closed her eyes and offered a prayer: *Be with the Millers, Lord, and if they're on the road with their horse and buggy, please keep them safe.*

Philadelphia

"I appreciate you coming with me today," Susan said as she and Luke entered a furniture store on the outskirts of the city. "Grandpa's old chair is getting pretty worn, so Anne and I want to get him a new one for Christmas." She smiled at Luke. "I really need a man's opinion."

He grinned back at her, and her heart nearly melted. Not counting Grandpa, she'd never felt so relaxed and contented with any man the way she did with Luke.

"I'm not sure how much help I'll be," he said, "but I can try out a few chairs and let you know which ones feel comfortable to me."

"That's all I want." Susan led the way through the store to the section where sofas, recliners, and rocking chairs were sold. "Here's a nice blue one." She motioned to a larger recliner. "Take a seat and tell me what you think."

Luke sat down and stood back up almost immediately. "That one's too big, and it wasn't very comfortable. The chair would swallow him up, I think."

"Okay. How about that one over there?" Susan pointed to a tan recliner that also rocked and swiveled.

Luke sat down, leaned his head back, and closed his eyes. He stayed like that for several minutes, causing her to wonder if he'd fallen asleep. Susan was about to give his arm a shake, when his eyes popped open. "This chair feels good to me. I think your grandpa would like it."

Susan smiled. She hadn't expected they

would find one so quickly. "Great! I'll talk to the salesman and see if I can put some money down on the chair and then pay the rest before Christmas. You can wait there if you like." She giggled. "Just don't fall asleep."

He wiggled his eyebrows playfully as he started to rock the chair. "I'll try not to."

Susan headed to the counter, where the salesman waited on another customer. When he was done, it didn't take him long to write up the paperwork for Susan's purchase. She returned to where she'd left Luke, but he wasn't there.

Susan glanced around and was relieved to see Luke standing beside a beautiful oak dining-room table that could have easily seated ten or twelve people. He was bent over, looking closely at the table, and rubbing his hand over the wood grain with an odd expression. "Luke, is something wrong?" she asked, approaching him.

He straightened and blinked his turquoise eyes. "I used to work in a furniture store."

As they got closer to Darby, Luke stared out the window of Susan's car, barely noticing the snowflakes coming down. All he could think about was the fact that he'd remembered having worked in a furniture store. But where was that store? Did he own it or work for someone else? Had he been a salesman there, or was he a woodworker who built some of the furniture?

Luke leaned his head back and closed his eyes. *Why can't I remember the details? Will my past ever come fully back to me?*

"Are you okay?" Susan asked, reaching across the seat to touch his arm.

"I'm fine. Just thinking, is all."

"About having worked in a furniture store?"

"Yeah. I wish the pieces would come to me. I'm tired of struggling to remember who I am," Luke murmured in frustration. "I know I should be happy that even a little bit is emerging about myself, but I get discouraged when I can't recall the rest of it."

"You know that your name is Luke, and I think you're on the verge of getting your memory completely back, so cling to that."

Susan sounded so sincere, Luke almost believed her. Maybe these little flashes of memory he kept having *were* a sign that he was on the threshold of remembering everything about his past.

"I can't believe how hard it's snowing; especially when it wasn't doing anything when we left home," Susan said, motioning to the heavy flakes hitting the front window. It looked as if they had the makings for a full-blown snowstorm. The windshield wipers could hardly keep up.

"I love the snow, but I don't like to drive in it," Susan said, her knuckles turning white as she gripped the steering wheel.

Luke wished he could offer to take over the driving, but he didn't know whether he'd ever driven a car. Besides, he didn't have a driver's license.

"I don't think the weatherman said anything about getting a lot of snow this morning," Susan observed. "He did say a few snow squalls could move through our area, and sometimes those squalls can give us a couple inches when all's said and done," she added.

Knowing she was nervous and wanting to keep the conversation light, Luke grinned at her and said, "Hey, if the snow keeps up like this, maybe we can build a snowman when we get home."

She nodded and seemed to relax a bit. "That sounds like fun."

Paradise

"Congratulations to both of you," Meredith said as she greeted her sister and new brother-in-law with a hug. "I hope you'll both be very happy."

"I know we will." Laurie's face beamed as she clung to her groom's hand.

A Vow for Always

Kevin smiled down at her. "With God at the center of our lives, every day will be an adventure." He nodded at Meredith. "I want you to know that I'll take good care of your sister."

She poked his arm playfully. "You'd better, or you'll have to answer to me."

"I sure wouldn't want that." He winked at Meredith.

"Where's Jonah?" Laurie asked. "I thought he and his folks were coming to the wedding."

"They were planning to," Meredith replied. "Something must have happened." It had started snowing during the ceremony, and now the roads were covered. She didn't voice her concerns to Laurie, but she was worried about Jonah. It wasn't like him to say he was going to do something and not follow through. Maybe he and his folks had been in an accident.

"We'd better go into the fellowship hall," Kevin said, smiling at Laurie. "Everyone's gathered for the reception."

Laurie giggled. "I think you're just anxious to eat some of that good food the women from your church have prepared."

He gave his stomach a thump. "What can I say? I'm a hungry man."

"Are you coming, Meredith?" Laurie asked.

Meredith nodded. "I'll be right behind you."

As the newlyweds headed down the stairs to the fellowship hall, Meredith thought about how

51

different from an Amish wedding their wedding service had been. Besides the fact that it had been held inside a church building, there would be just one meal following the service, not three, like in most traditional Amish weddings. That meant the festivities would be over much sooner.

Meredith was about to head down the stairs, when she caught sight of Merle Raber, who often drove Jonah and his folks places when they couldn't take their horse and buggy. He hurried toward Meredith with a grim expression. "Jonah asked me to come. He wanted me to tell you that he's sorry he couldn't make it to your sister's wedding."

"What's wrong?" Meredith asked, alarm welling up in her chest. "Did something happen to Jonah?"

Merle shook his head. "His dad got pinned under a buggy they'd been working on, and he's at the hospital getting checked over."

Meredith gasped. "That's terrible. I hope he isn't seriously hurt."

"I don't think so," Merle said, "but he was having a little trouble breathing, so they wanted to check him over real good."

"That makes sense," Meredith said with a nod. "Thank you for letting me know. I hope and pray that Raymond's okay."

A Vow for Always

Darby

"Are you going to come outside and help us build a snowman?" Susan asked Anne after she and Luke returned from their shopping trip.

Anne's curls bounced around her face as she shook her head. "You two go ahead. I just got off work, and I'm gonna curl up in front of the fireplace and finish reading that book I started last week."

"Is it another Amish-themed novel?" Susan asked.

Anne nodded. "I don't know why, but I'm fascinated with the Amish way of life."

Susan smiled. "Maybe we should make another trip to Lancaster when the weather warms in the spring. We can stop at one of the farmers' markets and see what else we might buy."

Anne bobbed her head. "Luke, maybe you'd like to go with us. We could go for a buggy ride, browse some of the shops, and eat shoofly pie."

Luke's eyebrows furrowed, and he rubbed his forehead. "I think I may have had shoofly pie before, but I can't remember where or what it tastes like."

"It has a molasses base," Susan said. "They sell it at the farmers' market in Philly. Maybe you had some there."

Luke shrugged. "Guess that could be. I'm just not sure. Fact is, I'm not sure about anything that took place before I woke up in the hospital and met you two."

Susan's heart ached for Luke. She could see by his pinched expression that he was struggling hard to remember his past. Maybe what he needed was a distraction. She pointed out the kitchen window, where the snow was coming down harder. "Why don't we head outside now and build that snowman before it gets too cold?"

"Sounds good to me. Let's go!" Luke grabbed Susan's hand, and they headed out the back door.

Once outside, they began rolling a snowball. Soon they had three good-sized balls and had formed a snowman. Then they put a carrot in for its nose, two matching rocks for the eyes, and placed Luke's red baseball cap on the snowman's head.

"He looks pretty good, don't you think?" Luke asked, standing back to admire their creation.

Susan nodded. "Let's make some snow angels now."

Luke chuckled when she dropped to the ground, spread her arms and legs, and moved them back and forth through the snow. When she hopped up, the place in the snow where she'd been flapping her arms looked like a pair of angel's wings.

Without warning, Susan scooped up a handful

of snow and flung it at Luke. He shivered when it landed on his neck. "Hey!"

Quickly, he leaned down and formed a snowball then tossed it at Susan. It landed on her right arm. "No fair, I wasn't ready for that!" She whirled around, but before she could take a step, Luke threw another clump of snow. This one hit Susan's shoulder.

Soon, there were snowballs flying back and forth, along with peals of laughter. Luke was having such a great time, he forgot about his earlier frustrations. It felt good to run around like a kid, enjoying the fresh-fallen snow while chasing Susan.

Luke watched slyly when Susan scooted behind a pine tree in one corner of the Baileys' yard. *What is she up to now?* he wondered. The white pine's soft needles were covered with snow, and several pinecones still clung to a few of the branches.

Luke glanced up and noticed a low-hanging limb right above where Susan stood behind the tree. *I'll get her now.* Luke smirked and whipped around to the other side of the tree. On impulse, he jumped up and shook the tree limb.

"Yikes!" Susan squealed as a wall of snow fell on her head. "I'll get you for that!" she warned, spitting snow from her mouth.

Before she could get the snow wiped from her face, Luke turned in the other direction, hoping to get out of the line of fire.

"You can't get away from me," Susan yelled with excitement in her voice.

Whap! Another snowball made its mark, sending icy cold fragments of snow down Luke's neck. He whirled around and raced after Susan, quickly grabbing her around the waist.

Panting and laughing, they fell to the ground in a heap of cold snow. As Luke lay there beside her, huffing and puffing, his gaze went to her rosy-red lips. Seeing the merriment in Susan's eyes, he leaned closer as the urge to kiss her became strong. His lips were mere inches from hers, when the back door opened and Anne shouted, "Hey, you two! Why don't you come inside and warm up with a cup of hot chocolate and some of Grandma's melt-in-your-mouth banana bread?"

Luke looked at Susan to get her reaction. Was that a look of disappointment on her face? Had she been hoping he would kiss her? Did she want it as much as he did?

Maybe it's best that we were interrupted, he thought. *Since I haven't put the pieces of my past together yet, I really can't commit to Susan right now.*

Luke's growing attraction to her made him even more anxious to know his past. If he could just find the key to unlock the memories hidden away in his head, he might feel free to express his feelings.

CHAPTER 5

Ronks

"I'm glad your daed wasn't seriously hurt," Meredith told Jonah as they sat on the sofa together in her parents' living room.

He nodded solemnly. "It about scared me to death when I found him pinned under the buggy like that. Fortunately the only injuries involved some bruising."

"God was watching over him," Meredith said.

Jonah nodded. "I would say so."

"When you didn't show up for Laurie and Kevin's wedding yesterday, I was worried— especially after seeing the snow come down as hard as it did."

"Well, it wasn't because of the weather, but we did feel bad about missing the wedding." He glanced around. "Where is everyone this evening? I expected to see your sisters and brothers running around like they usually do when I drop by."

"They're upstairs in their rooms," Meredith replied. "Dad thought it would be nice if we had some time alone, without the little ones climbing all over you."

Jonah chuckled. "They do seem to like me for some reason."

"That's because you're such a nice man, and they like those twisty animal balloons you make for them." Meredith smiled. "You're good with Levi, too. He lights up whenever you're in the room."

"He's a special little guy. I have a fondness for him, just like I do his mamm."

Meredith's cheeks warmed. "I have a fondness for you, too, Jonah."

"Enough to marry me in the spring?" he blurted unexpectedly.

She flinched and sucked in her breath, unsure of how to respond.

Jonah took her hand and gave her fingers a gentle squeeze. "I'm sorry for blurting that out. I'd planned to wait till you'd been widowed a year before I said anything about marriage, but the words just popped out of my mouth. Did I speak out of turn?" he asked.

She shook her head. "It's not that. I just need some time to think about it. Can you wait until Christmas for my answer?"

Slowly, he nodded.

A Vow for Always

Darby

"Where's Luke?" Susan asked when she entered the kitchen and found her grandmother fixing lunch.

"He and your grandpa are outside, shoveling snow off the driveway so you and Anne can get your cars out of the garage. It's a good thing you both have afternoon shifts, because the roads should be cleared by then."

Susan smiled. "Luke's thoughtful, isn't he, Grandma?"

Grandma nodded and reached for the loaf of bread sitting on the counter. "I heard him tell your grandpa the other day that he feels like he's imposing on us."

"What'd Grandpa say in response?"

"He told Luke in no uncertain terms that it's been a blessing to us having him here, and he should quit worrying so much."

"I hope Luke listened to him," Susan said. "I wouldn't want him to leave and go out on the streets."

Grandma tipped her head. "What makes you think he used to live on the streets?"

"I'm not sure if he did or not, but if he were to leave here, I'd be concerned about where he would go."

Grandma gave Susan's shoulder a squeeze. "Don't worry, honey, we won't let him leave. At least not until he gets his memory fully back and we find out where he came from."

Susan swallowed around the lump in her throat. "I'll miss him when that happens."

"You've fallen in love with Luke, haven't you, dear?"

Susan nodded slowly, her eyes filling with tears. She turned and looked out the window toward the pine tree in the far end of the yard. The tracks in the snow were still there, where she had hid from Luke when they'd played around in the snow. She smiled, despite her tears, remembering the cold bath she'd gotten when Luke snuck up from behind and knocked all the snow off the branch above her head. "Last night, when Luke and I were romping in the snow, I think he was on the verge of kissing me," she said.

"Why didn't he?" Grandma questioned.

"Anne came out and called us in for hot chocolate." Susan sniffed, hoping to keep her tears from spilling over. "Maybe it's a good thing we were interrupted. If Luke had kissed me, it would have strengthened our relationship even more, and I really don't want that right now. At least not until I know more about him."

"Is it because you fear he might already have a girlfriend, or maybe a wife?"

"Yeah. If I allow myself to think about a future between me and Luke, and then he remembers his life before and it includes someone else, I'd be devastated."

Grandma slipped her arm around Susan's waist and gave her a hug. "Just pray about it, honey. God will work it all out."

Ronks

Meredith yawned. She was more tired than usual as she got ready for bed. With the Christmas holiday approaching, she'd been getting more requests for prayer coverings to be made for the store where she'd been taking them. She would have to buckle down during the next couple of days and try to make a few extra. That, and Laurie's wedding with all of its preparations, plus Thanksgiving, had kept her on the go.

On top of that, worrying over where Jonah and his family had been when they didn't show up at the wedding, and then Jonah suddenly asking her to marry him had only added to her fatigue.

"No wonder I'm exhausted," she mused, looking at Fritz lying in his usual spot on the floor by the foot of her bed.

The dog looked up at her, with all four legs

stretched out to one side. From the way he was lying, his short tail was just long enough to make little thumping sounds as he wagged it against the floor.

"You look tired, too, pup," Meredith said.

Fritz offered a whiney groan before he laid his head down, looking toward the door. Ever since they'd moved back in with her parents, Fritz had been getting more exercise each day, playing with Freckles, the Kings' new family pet. Meredith was glad the dogs got along well; it was one less thing for her to worry about.

As tired as she was, Meredith could tell she wouldn't be falling asleep any time soon. Lying down with her hands behind her head on the fluffy, down-filled pillow, she pondered Jonah's speedy proposal. Truthfully speaking, it wasn't really such a surprise that Jonah had proposed. Meredith had been expecting it, just not this evening. She'd figured he would wait until she'd been widowed at least a full year.

"Am I ready for this?" Meredith spoke out loud into the darkness of her room. Listening to her son's even breathing coming from the crib across the room, and to Fritz's contented snoring from the floor by her bed, Meredith was glad she hadn't awakened either of them. "Wish I could be asleep like the two of you are right now," she whispered.

Meredith couldn't help being excited about

the upcoming holidays. She and Jonah had several things planned besides the usual family gatherings that she was anxious to partake in. Meredith sighed, pulling the quilt up and tucking it under her chin. Christmas was the last holiday she'd spent with Luke before he'd been killed. After that, she hadn't thought she'd enjoy another Christmas. Nor much else, for that matter. But Jonah had proven her wrong.

As she lay staring at the ceiling, Meredith realized that her relationship with Jonah had become more comfortable. She was at ease when he was around. Levi also seemed to gravitate toward Jonah. Meredith's family had accepted him as if he were already part of the family. Even Luke's parents seemed adjusted to the idea of Jonah courting their daughter-in-law. But would the family's acceptance be enough?

As the stillness of the night enveloped the house, Meredith wondered, *Oh, Luke, what should I do?*

CHAPTER 6

Ronks

It was kind of Jonah's folks to invite us to their house for Christmas dinner," Meredith's mother said as they put their fresh-baked pumpkin and apple pies into boxes.

Meredith smiled. "Jah, it'll be a nice afternoon out, and you won't have to cook for a change."

"I don't mind cooking. Never have—not even when I was a *maedel*."

"How old were you when Grandma taught you to cook?" Meredith asked, closing the lid on the box of pies.

"Let's see now. . .for as long as I can remember I enjoyed being in the kitchen, helping my mamm with whatever she would allow me to do."

"That's right," Grandma Smucker spoke up from across the room, where she'd been cutting apples, pears, and bananas for a fruit salad she'd be taking to the Millers.' "By the time Luann was born, her sisters were already in school. So she pretty much followed me everywhere around the house. And since I spent a good deal of time in the kitchen, she was there, too, always asking to help." Grandma smiled. "By the time your mamm was six years old, she was baking cookies."

While Mom and Grandma continued to reminisce about old times, Meredith walked into the living room and looked out the window. Squinting at the bright sunlight hitting the sparkly white snow, she gazed at the beautiful, almost magical scene.

Christmas made her feel more spirited and full of life, and a snowfall close to the holiday made her seem even more energized. It was fun to watch Arlene, Katie, and Owen, her youngest siblings, romping in the snow. It was like someone flipped a switch on their energy level, taking it up a notch. Any other time, their liveliness would have gotten on Meredith's nerves, but she had to admit, she was feeling their excitement as well.

All week, Meredith had heard Mom and Grandma Smucker humming as they baked. Even Dad and her brother Stanley didn't seem to mind the cold as they tended the animals and worked in the barn. To free Mom up for her extra baking, Kendra and Nina had pitched in to help mind the kids and keep the house nice and tidy. Meredith didn't let the idea of her sister Laurie moving away soon get in the way of the joy she felt.

Meredith had promised to give Jonah an answer to his proposal later today, and as the time drew closer for them to load up their buggies and head for the Millers', she found herself feeling anxious to get there. She'd lain awake for several hours last night, praying and trying to decide what her answer should be. In the wee hours of the morning, Meredith's answer finally came, and she felt a sense of peace.

Bird-in-Hand

"Would everyone like dessert now, or should we let our meal settle a bit?" Jonah's mother, Sarah, asked after everyone had finishing eating.

"I can't speak for anyone else," Meredith's dad said, pushing back his chair, "but right now I couldn't eat another bite."

"Me neither," Jonah agreed. "In fact, I was thinking of taking Meredith on a sleigh ride." He glanced at Meredith and smiled. "How about it? Would you care to join me?"

Meredith hesitated. If she took a ride with Jonah, it would give her the chance to give him her answer about marrying him. However, as much as Meredith wanted to go, she didn't feel right about leaving the other women to do the dishes. She was about to say so and start clearing the table, when Sarah scooped up several plates and said, "Don't concern yourself with that, Meredith. There are enough of us here to get the dishes done, so feel free to join Jonah outside and take advantage of that fresh air. Who knows how long this snow will stick around or when the next snowfall might be?"

"Don't worry about Levi, either," Meredith's sixteen-year-old sister, Kendra, was quick to say. "If he wakes up from his nap, I'll keep him occupied."

"And if she doesn't, I will," Dad added with a wink. "I never mind holding my grandson."

"Everyone in our family enjoys holding Levi," Grandma Smucker added. "He's such a sweet boppli."

"Shall we get our coats?" Jonah asked, motioning to the jackets hanging on the wall pegs in the utility room.

Meredith nodded and rose to her feet. "Let me tend to Levi first, and I'll be with you in a few minutes."

When they stepped outside a short time later, Meredith sucked in her breath. "It's been such a lovely day, Jonah. See how the snow glistens?"

"Jah, it's beautiful," Jonah whispered, leaning

close to her ear. "Pretty as a picture, just like you."

Meredith shivered, feeling his breath blow against her ear. Hearing his laughter as he skipped over the last two porch steps and jumped into the snow, she, too, felt lighthearted. Then, as he beckoned her to follow, she went quickly down the porch steps and out into the yard.

"All I have to do is hitch Dobbin to the sleigh, and we'll be on our way," Jonah said. "Dad's horse is more accustomed to pulling a sleigh."

Before Meredith knew it, they were heading over the back fields and breaking through new snow. The only disturbances they could see in the snow were a few animal tracks and areas where deer had pawed away the snow, uncovering vegetation to eat.

During the ride, they laughed, visited, and watched the sun set in the west. Meredith enjoyed listening to the sound of the sleigh bells. Hearing them brought back happy childhood memories when Dad used to take the family on winter sleigh rides.

"Are you warm enough?" Jonah asked, looking over at Meredith.

"I'm fine. It's warm and toasty under this thick wool blanket." She smiled, noticing how relaxed Jonah seemed to be, loosely holding the reins. He was obviously having as much fun as she was.

"Look over there!" Jonah pointed across the

way. Four deer stood warily watching near a clump of trees, but as the sleigh approached, they turned and ran over the hill.

When the sleigh reached the knoll, Jonah halted the horse. Dobbin pawed the ground a few times as the steam puffed out of his nose and rose off his rich auburn coat. Meredith looked at the view and thought she'd never seen a prettier sight. The blanket of snow gave everything a quiet look, as stillness lay over the land. Smoke coming from chimneys hung heavy in the air, and silos stood tall and visible in every direction.

Jonah reached for Meredith's hand and held it firmly in his. "Meredith, I was wondering if you've had enough time to think about my marriage proposal."

She nodded slowly. "I have, Jonah, and I will marry you."

His face broke into a wide smile. "Now that's the best Christmas present I could ever receive!"

She giggled as Jonah jumped out of the sleigh, ran around to her side, picked her up, and twirled her around. Dobbin whinnied, pawed at the ground some more, and nodded his head as though in agreement. "I was thinking we could be married in early March, if that's all right with you," Meredith said as he gently set her on her feet.

"I wish it could be sooner, but I have no problem with March." Jonah leaned close, and she thought he might kiss her. Instead, he reached for her hand and gave it a squeeze.

"I don't think we should tell anyone yet," Meredith said. "I'd feel better about waiting until my year of mourning is up."

Jonah's smile faded. "Not even our folks? Don't you think we ought to tell them now?"

Meredith shook her head. "I'd rather wait."

Although disappointed, Jonah smiled and said, "Whatever you think is best."

Darby

"You three women certainly outdid yourselves preparing this meal," Henry said, giving his stomach a thump. "I think every year Christmas dinner tastes better."

"Thank you, Grandpa," Susan spoke up, "but Grandma did most of the cooking."

"That's not true," Grandma said, handing Susan the platter of juicy ham. "You mashed the potatoes, and Anne made the fruit salad."

"That's right, Grandma," Anne said in a teasing tone. "Susan likes to lick the beaters when she's done mashing the potatoes. But you prepared everything else."

Grandpa smiled. "That's 'cause my wife likes to cook."

A Vow for Always

"That's right, I do, and you like to eat my cooking." Grandma chuckled and poked Grandpa's arm playfully. "I've had lots of practice over the years to perfect my cooking skills."

Grandpa forked a piece of ham into his mouth. "Mmm. . .this is so good. Don't you think so, son?" he asked, looking at Luke as he took a bite of the bright red cherry and pineapple ring that had been on top of the glaze, adding flavor to the ham.

Luke nodded.

Susan pursed her lips. It wasn't like Luke to be so quiet. Normally he was quite talkative during a meal. At least that's how he'd been the last couple of months. He'd joined in the conversation early today, too, when everyone had opened their presents.

Susan had been pleased to see how well Grandpa liked the chair she and Luke had picked out for him, and Grandma said she appreciated the Crock-Pot, sweater, and perfume the girls had given her, too. Luke had even made gifts for everyone—a "WELCOME TO OUR HOME" plaque for Grandma, a feeder for George the squirrel for Grandpa, and jewelry boxes for Anne and Susan, all of which he'd managed to make when no one was around. They'd given something to Luke as well: a nicely framed photograph of the four of them. Grandpa said it was so Luke could always remember them.

Could Luke be thinking about his past—maybe wondering what he'd been doing last Christmas, and who he was with? If that's what he was thinking, Susan couldn't blame him. She'd be doing the same thing if she were in his situation. In fact, such questions would probably be constantly on her mind.

Maybe Luke's hoping for a Christmas miracle, Susan thought. *Oh, I wish I could give him the gift of getting his memory back.* If there were any extra miracles to be given, she hoped with all her heart that Luke would regain his past life.

CHAPTER 7

Ronks

$\mathcal{B}$y the end of January, Meredith felt ready to announce her engagement but wanted Jonah to be with her. So they'd decided to have a joint family dinner where they could share their good news.

Too bad Laurie and Kevin won't be here, Meredith thought as she set the table. They'd left the first week of January for Missouri, where they were ministering to a Native American community. In Laurie's last letter, she'd described how much she and Kevin were enjoying their life together and said that working with kids during several church events had made them eager to have children of their own. She'd also mentioned how good it felt to help the elderly with transportation to and from their doctors' appointments.

Meredith smiled. Laurie sounded happy and

would be a wonderful mother someday. It would be nice for Levi to have a little cousin to play with, but they might not get to see each other much, with Laurie and Kevin going on missionary trips. Well, at least her son would have his uncles and aunts to shower him with attention, not to mention the love he would continue to get from his doting grandparents. Meredith's siblings, especially the younger ones, loved spending time with Levi. In fact, Katie, Arlene, and Owen were keeping him entertained in the living room while she prepared dinner.

"Is there anything I can do to help you?" Grandma Smucker asked.

"No, thanks, Grandma. I told Mom a few minutes ago to relax in the living room with the kinner and that I had everything under control, so you ought to do the same."

Grandma slipped her arm around Meredith's waist. "You look well rested and happier than I've seen you in a long time. Is there something going on we should know about?"

Meredith's face heated with embarrassment. Was her excitement really that obvious? "I'm just happy to be able to serve my family a nice meal this evening," she said, avoiding her grandmother's question.

Grandma studied Meredith. "I notice you're not wearing black today. It's nice to see you in that blue dress."

Meredith glanced down at her dress and matching apron. "Luke has been gone a year now, Grandma, so it was time for me to put my mourning clothes aside."

Grandma smiled with a knowing expression. "And it's good to see that you're moving on with your life." Did she suspect that Meredith was planning to marry Jonah? The whole family probably suspected what was going on. After all, Jonah visited her a lot these days, and everyone knew they were courting. In any event, Meredith was confident that everyone would be happy for them and offer their blessings.

As Jonah sat beside Meredith on one side of the Kings' dining-room table that evening, his palms grew sweaty. *When should I make the announcement?* he wondered. *Should I tell them during dinner while we're eating? Or would it be better to wait till we're eating dessert?*

Jonah felt like a silly schoolboy. How would he say it? He hadn't even prepared a speech. Should he tell everyone, kids included, or should he and Meredith take their parents aside and only announce it to them for now?

No, he decided. *We should tell everyone at once. Maybe now would be a good time.*

Jonah cleared his throat and wiped his sweaty

brow. A shiver ran through him. Why was he so nervous, for goodness' sake?

"Are you okay, Son?" Dad asked. "You look like you're not feeling so well."

"I–I'm fine," Jonah stammered.

Meredith, as if sensing his predicament, tapped her water glass with her fork and said, "Jonah and I have an announcement to make."

All heads turned in their direction.

She looked over at Jonah and gave him a reassuring smile, then she said in a clear tone, "Jonah asked me to marry him, and I said yes. We plan to get married in March."

Jonah held his breath, waiting for the response.

"Congratulations!" the Kings and his parents said. "That's great news," Meredith's father added. And the smiles around the table showed Jonah that everyone agreed.

Darby

"What a beautiful night for stargazing," Susan said as she and Luke took seats on the Baileys' back porch.

"You're right," Luke murmured, staring up at the sky. "The sky's so clear I can see most of the constellations."

They sat in quiet camaraderie for several

minutes, and then Luke reached over and took Susan's hand. She looked at him and smiled. He didn't know why, but he felt like he'd done this before —maybe in his previous life with someone else. It was very disconcerting and seemed all too familiar. Maybe he was just remembering a few months back, when one evening he and Susan had watched for falling stars. They stayed that way awhile longer, then Luke shivered and said, "Sure is cold out tonight. It felt really cold like this before I got on the bus, too."

"What bus?" Susan questioned, tipping her head and staring at him.

He shrugged. "I don't know. Just remember being cold and riding on a bus." He groaned as he leaned forward and cradled his head in his hands. "This not being able to remember things about my past is nearly driving me crazy. It's kind of like trying to put together a difficult jigsaw puzzle and nothing seems to fit."

"I know it has to be hard," Susan said, gently squeezing his arm. "But you're remembering a few more things all the time, like just now when you remembered getting on a bus." She paused. "You had to be going somewhere, Luke, because you were found badly beaten in the Philadelphia bus station."

He lifted his head and offered her a weak smile. "I wonder what I did to make someone mad enough to beat me up."

"Maybe you didn't do anything," Susan said in a reassuring tone. "It might have been some maniac who just liked to push people around." Her expression sobered. "Or maybe the person responsible for your injuries needed money, and when you said no, he beat you up and took your wallet. Remember, there was no wallet or any identification found on you, Luke."

He shook his head forcibly. "No, I don't remember. If I did, I wouldn't be here right now, trying to put the pieces of my life together." Frustration welled in Luke's chest, and he fought to keep his emotions in check.

"I'm sorry. I didn't mean to upset you," she said. "I guess I didn't word things quite right. What I meant to say was, remember what I told you the police said to those they spoke to at the hospital when they brought you in?"

"Yeah, I know what you told me, but it's not the same as me actually remembering what happened in that bus station."

"Luke, I have an idea."

"What's that?"

"Do you think it might help you remember if we went to the bus station where you were found?" she suggested.

"I don't know. Guess it's worth a try."

"All right then, we'll take a ride over there on my next day off."

Sometimes Luke couldn't get over how

sweet and accommodating Susan was. He was falling harder for her all the time and wished he could express his feelings. But that would have to wait until he knew for sure who he was and what had transpired in his past.

CHAPTER 8

Ronks

When Meredith looked at the kitchen calendar on the second Monday of March, she couldn't believe it. In just three days, she and Jonah would be married.

A few weeks ago, Jonah had taken Meredith to see a farm he hoped to buy. He'd put money down on the place, and if all went well, the deal would close the day before their wedding. Jonah had put away sizeable savings from working in Ohio and then with his Dad. He'd wanted to use the money toward buying a place when the time came for him to marry. With Jonah's job, plus the rent money they would receive from Meredith's house, they should be able to live quite comfortably. Everything seemed to be falling into place, and she was almost sure that marrying Jonah was the right thing to do. Why then, did she feel a sense of apprehension this morning?

Staring out the window, as her breath steamed the glass, Meredith looked beyond the yard and into the fields. She pictured the day a little over a year ago when she and Luke had been eating breakfast and talking about the business offer Luke had gotten from his uncle in Indiana.

Meredith sighed, resting her forehead against the cool window, as she remembered how her suspicions had been true of being pregnant with her and Luke's firstborn. With the window still fogged over from her warm breath, she drew a happy face with her finger. She had been blessed in so many aspects of her life. Looking up, she said a brief prayer of thanks for the time, however short, that she'd had with Luke, and now their most precious gift, little Levi.

"*Guder mariye*," Mom said, entering the kitchen. "Did you sleep well last night?"

"Good morning," Meredith replied, turning away from the window. "I slept okay. How about you?"

"With your daed's snoring and the incessant howling of the wind, I didn't sleep so well," Mom admitted.

"I'm sorry to hear that."

Mom yawned. "It's okay; I'll catch a catnap this afternoon and be good as new."

She moved across the room to the propane

stove and picked up the teakettle. "Are you getting *naerfich* about the wedding?" she asked, filling the teakettle.

"Not really nervous; just kind of anxious is all," Meredith replied. "But I guess that's to be expected when one is about to get married."

"Were you anxious before you married Luke?"

"Not really. I was excited and couldn't wait to be his bride."

Mom set the teakettle on the stove and moved to stand beside Meredith. "Are you sure you're doing the right thing marrying Jonah?"

Meredith stiffened. "I thought you liked Jonah and had given us your blessing."

"I do like him, and so does your daed. I'm just concerned that you might be rushing into things."

Meredith shook her head vigorously. "I'm not. Jonah will be a good husband to me, and an equally good daed to Levi."

"I'm sure that's true, but if you're feeling—"

"I'll be fine, really. It's just a bit of pre-wedding jitters."

Bird-in-Hand

"I think I ate too much," Jonah said, pushing away from the table. "Danki, Mom, for fixing such a tasty breakfast."

"Jah," Dad agreed. "The ham and eggs were real good."

Jonah rose to his feet and went to get the coffeepot. After he'd poured himself a second cup of coffee, he sat back down and listened as his folks talked about the buggy business and the strong March winds they'd been having.

Leaning back in his chair, Jonah's thoughts went to Meredith. In just a few days his dream of settling down with someone he loved would begin. Who knew that his teenage friend from years ago would one day become his bride? Meredith was everything he'd ever hoped for in a wife. He admired her parents and the close relationship they had, and looked forward to becoming part of that family as much as he longed for Meredith and Levi to be a part of his.

Jonah smiled, thinking about the other night when he'd stopped by to see Meredith. He'd watched Levi sleeping soundly in his mother's arms and felt overwhelmed with the love he had for that precious little boy. The deep abiding love he felt for Levi's mother was something Jonah had only wished for before. Now it was a reality, and he felt confident that Meredith loved him, too. Maybe not in the same way she'd loved her first husband, but he was certain her feelings were genuine. Jonah looked forward to becoming a father, not only to Levi, but to any other children he and Meredith might be blessed with.

"So what do you think, Son?" Mom asked, breaking into Jonah's thoughts.

Jonah jerked, nearly spilling his cup of coffee. "Uh—about what?"

"About the weather," Dad said before Mom could reply. "Do you think this awful wind we've been having will let up any time soon?"

Jonah shrugged. "I have no idea, Dad. I wasn't even thinkin' about the weather."

Mom poked Jonah's arm playfully. "That's because your mind was someplace else, and I bet I know where. You were thinking about your upcoming wedding, am I right?"

Jonah gave a nod.

"Are you naerfich?" Dad asked.

"No. Well, I guess maybe I am," Jonah admitted. "I want everything to be perfect, but more than that, I hope I can be the kind of husband Meredith needs and a good daed to Levi."

Mom patted his hand affectionately. "You will be, Son. I have no doubt of that."

Darby

"What's in there?" Grandpa asked when Susan took her seat at the breakfast table beside Luke.

She smiled, placing a small box on the extra chair in the corner behind her. "It's a present for one of my patients."

"Which patient is that?" Grandma asked, sipping her tea.

"A five-year-old girl named Elsie. She and her parents were in a car accident." Susan took a piece of toast and slathered it with Grandma's homemade apple butter. "The poor little thing has a broken arm, several nasty cuts and bruises, and she suffered a severe blow to her head."

"That's a shame," said Anne. "Is she in stable condition?"

"She's getting better," Susan replied. "But she doesn't say much, and I thought it might cheer her up if she had a doll to cuddle. So I decided to give her the little faceless doll I bought at the farmers' market last year." She leaned her chair back and pulled the doll out of the box.

"That's what I've been seeing in these dreams I keep having," Luke said. "At first I thought it was faceless people, but I think it's a doll like this one." He touched the doll where it's face would have been, staring at it as though in disbelief. "Someone I know had a doll like this."

"Who was it, Luke?" Grandpa asked, leaning close to Luke.

Luke made little circles across his forehead with his fingertips. "I think her name was Laura. No, maybe not. It started with an *L*, though; I'm pretty sure of that."

"Think of some *L* names," Grandma said, coaxing Luke.

He studied the faceless doll. "Laurie! Her name was Laurie, and she had a doll like this. No, not one doll, but several."

"Susan, wasn't that young woman at the farmers' market who sold you the doll named Laurie?" Anne spoke up.

"Yes, I think it was." Susan turned to face Luke. "Have you ever been to the farmers' market in Bird-in-Hand?"

His eyes widened. "I believe I have."

Grandpa reached over and clasped Luke's arm. "I wonder if you might be Amish."

The look of astonishment on Luke's face told Susan the answer.

CHAPTER 9

The following evening, Luke watched nervously as Anne and Susan searched the Internet, looking for Amish last names. He had never heard the word "Google" before and quickly learned it meant doing a search for information on the computer. He sipped at his hot tea, watching in amazement at what the computer could do.

Susan glanced over at him and smiled. "I'm sure this is all new to you, Luke, but we use computers for just about everything these days. Especially at the hospital."

Luke shook his head, still dumfounded as Susan added, "Just about anything you want to know can be accessed by the click of a button, as long as you know the right words to search for."

After checking out several websites that didn't help much, they finally found one that listed Amish last names. They started reading the long list out loud. When they got to "Stoltzfus," Luke immediately knew who he was. His name was Luke Stoltzfus, and he was Amish!

His hand went to his forehead, as more memories came flooding back. "I have a wife, and her name is Merrie. We have a home somewhere in Lancaster County, but I'm not sure where." It made no sense that Luke could remember some things and not others.

"So if I live in Lancaster, how and why did I end up in Philadelphia?" he asked Susan, who sat quietly by his side at the kitchen table. "Why was I at that bus station?"

He and Susan had gone there several weeks ago, but it had done nothing to spark any memories.

"I don't know," she said, slowly shaking her head. "But with your memory coming back this quickly, I'm sure that information will come to you eventually, too."

"My name is Luke Stoltzfus," he repeated over and over. It was like music to his ears. He felt like a real person; he was somebody, at last!

He looked back at Susan and noticed that her shoulders were slumped as she took their empty teacups to the sink. Wasn't she happy his memory was coming back?

"It's getting late," Anne said, turning off the computer. "I think we should all go to bed and continue with this in the morning."

"My sister's right," Susan was quick to say. "After a good night's sleep, your brain will be rested, and it'll help you remember more."

Luke nodded. "Jah, maybe so."

"Jah?" Susan asked, looking at him curiously.

He grinned. "It's the way the Amish say yes. It's funny I've never said it till now, though. If I'm Amish, wouldn't you think I'd have been speaking Pennsylvania-Dutch?"

"Not when you had amnesia," Anne said. "Until recently, it was as though your past had been completely erased from your brain."

"Tomorrow, hopefully, I'll remember my phone number—if I have one that is," Luke quickly added. He pushed away from the table and left the room, feeling tired yet exhilarated. He could hardly believe he'd remembered so much of his past in one evening. He was ever so anxious to get back to Meredith. Now all he needed to do was remember his phone number and address.

"Whew!" Anne blew out her breath. "Can you believe how quickly things started coming together for Luke once he saw your Amish doll?"

"I know." Susan stared at a stain on the tablecloth as a lump formed in her throat. She'd known from the beginning that Luke's time with them had been uncertain and that his memory could come back at any moment. She just hadn't been prepared to fall in love with him; and learning that he had a wife had been a harsh blow.

So much for my fantasies about building a life together with Luke, she thought. Tears welled in Susan's eyes and ran down her cheeks. *I'm being selfish*, she chastised herself. *I should be happy that Luke will be getting his life back with the woman he married, but I know I'll miss the "Eddie" I once knew.*

Ronks

After another restless night, Luann got up before anyone else in order to get a few things done. With just one day before Meredith's wedding, she still had a lot to do.

Her gaze came to rest on the tablecloth waiting to be wrapped. It had been a wedding gift she and Philip had received from his folks. Luann wished her father and Philip's parents were still alive. They'd all loved being included in family gatherings.

Pulling her thoughts back to the issue at hand, Luann quickly wrapped the present so that Meredith wouldn't see it when she got up. She reviewed the menu for the wedding meal: roasted chicken, mashed potatoes and gravy, a fruit salad, creamed celery, cheese, bologna, bread, butter, honey, jelly, fruits, pudding, cakes, and pies—plenty of good food for all their guests.

Her thoughts returned to Meredith. She'd chosen a dark green fabric for her wedding dress and had made it in a day. Of course, she was an excellent seamstress and had caught on to sewing at an early age. It was no wonder she was able to sew women's prayer coverings with such ease. Unfortunately, it hadn't given Meredith enough income, and she'd had to rent out her home.

Luann had told only Philip that she was concerned Meredith might be marrying Jonah, at least in part, for financial reasons. She knew Meredith felt like a burden for having to move in with her family. Luann's biggest concern, however, was that Meredith might not be over the pain of losing Luke, and if that was the case, it could affect her marriage to Jonah.

At least Luke's parents had accepted the idea of Meredith getting married again. Even so, it would be hard for them to attend the wedding and see their daughter-in-law marry another man.

Luann glanced out the window. The sky was gray, threatening to unleash the drizzle that had been predicted. She hoped the weather would clear by Thursday.

"I just need to relax and stop fretting about things," she murmured. "Meredith's life is in

God's hands, and so is the weather. May His will be done."

Darby

Luke sat up in bed with a start. He remembered his phone number. After quickly writing it down, he hurried to get dressed, anxious to tell the Baileys this good news.

"Guess what?" he shouted, sliding across the kitchen floor in his stocking feet a short time later.

"What's up?" Henry asked from his place at the table, where he sat drinking coffee. "You look like George when he's swiped some seed from one of our birdfeeders."

"I remember my phone number," Luke said excitedly.

"That's wonderful, Luke," Norma said, joining them at the table.

"Are you going to call your wife or just surprise her by showing up?" Anne asked, placing a cup of coffee in front of Luke.

"I don't know. What do you think I should do?" Luke didn't know why he felt so confused. Everything seemed to be happening so fast, and yet he still couldn't quite remember some details—like how long he'd been gone or what he'd been doing at the bus station in Philadelphia. Maybe it wasn't important. Maybe he should just find a way home to Meredith as quickly as possible. But he couldn't really do that until he remembered exactly where he lived. All he knew was that he lived in Lancaster County, and he wasn't even sure what town.

"I think you should call your wife right away," Susan said, entering the room. Her eyes were red and swollen. Luke wondered if she might have been crying.

"Are you all right, dear?" Norma asked. "You look as if you've been—"

"I'm fine." Susan moved over to the desk, picked up the cordless phone, and handed it to Luke. "You'd better make that call now, don't you think?"

Luke slowly nodded. A chill of nervous anticipation ran through him as he quickly entered the number. It rang several times, then a recorded message came on, saying the number had been disconnected. He hung up, feeling defeated. He'd thought sure the phone number had to be his, but his memory was still sketchy about certain things, so maybe he'd been wrong. "All I got was a recording," he mumbled. "The number's been disconnected."

"Maybe you dialed incorrectly or had the wrong number in the first place," Henry spoke up. "Why don't you try again?"

Luke dialed the number once more and got the same message. "It's no use," he said with a groan. "It can't be my phone number."

Norma stood in front of Luke and put her hands on his shoulders. "Don't worry, Luke. Once you remember your address, you can surprise your wife in person. It might be better that way."

"Let's have breakfast first," Henry said. "Then we'll get things figured out. You'll be home before you know it."

The Baileys' optimism gave Luke a sense of hope. Maybe by this time tomorrow, he and Meredith would be reunited. Of course, he first had to remember exactly where he lived in Lancaster County.

CHAPTER 10

Bird-in-Hand

As Jonah prepared for bed the night before his wedding, he prayed that all would go well and that the weather would turn sunny. It could rain all it wanted tonight, but hopefully by morning it would clear out and start to dry things off so that his and Meredith's wedding would be perfect. Of course once tomorrow arrived, he probably wouldn't care what it was like outside.

All Jonah wanted was to begin a new life with Meredith and Levi, and even though the house he'd wanted to buy had suddenly been taken off the market, he'd be content to live with his folks a bit longer until he found another place. Meredith got along well with his parents, so he didn't think she'd mind living here awhile either. They could move into the house Meredith had shared with her first husband, but that wouldn't seem right—

at least not to Jonah. He didn't think Meredith needed the reminders from her past, and living in the home she'd shared with Luke might come between them. Maybe after he and Meredith were married she would decide to sell the house. After all, there wasn't much point in keeping it. She'd probably make more in the long run by selling the place than if she kept renting it out.

That can all be worked out down the road, Jonah told himself as he climbed into bed. *What I need now is a good night's sleep so I'll be well rested in the morning.* He turned down the gas lamp and closed his eyes. The last thing he remembered before drifting off to sleep was a vision of Meredith standing beside him, responding to her wedding vows.

Darby

Luke had spent most of the day trying to remember his address. He'd almost given up when, shortly before bedtime, it came to him. "I know where I live!" he shouted, dashing into the living room, where the Baileys sat, drinking hot chocolate.

"You do? Where?" Henry asked, rising to his feet.

"It's crazy how it all of a sudden came to me," Luke said in amazement. "I was flipping through the pages of a tree magazine you got the other day. You know—the one that also has flowers and vegetables you can send off for."

"Yes, I've ordered a few things from that catalog over the years," Norma said. "But tell us, Luke, how did that help you remember your address?"

"Well, I was reading about a beech tree, and I suddenly remembered the name of the road where my wife and I lived. We live on a farm on Beechdale Road in Bird-in-Hand, just off Route 340." He started pacing the floor, nervously running his fingers through his hair. "I need to go home now. Would it be possible for me to borrow enough money from you for a bus ticket to Lancaster?" he asked, looking at Henry. "I'll pay you back as soon as I can."

Henry shook his head. "No way, Luke. We'll drive you home; we wouldn't want it any other way."

"Really? When?" Even though Luke was excited to get home, he felt a touch of sorrow in his heart that he would be leaving these wonderful people who had opened their arms and shared a piece of their life with him.

"Let's go tonight," Susan said. "I don't have to work tomorrow, so I can take you there now."

"You would do that for me?" Luke could hardly believe Susan would offer to drive him home. They were a good hour and a half from Lancaster, and by the time they got there, it would be midnight or later.

"Of course I'll do it. That's what friends are for," she replied.

Luke noticed tears in Susan's eyes. Could it be that she would miss him? Had she been experiencing the same feelings for him as he had for her?

Good grief, Luke thought, rubbing his forehead. *I'm a married man in love with my wife, yet I almost allowed myself to fall in love with Susan. What would have happened if I had? What if I'd made a commitment to her?*

"I start work early in the morning, so I can't go along," Anne said. "But I want you to know that it's been a pleasure to know you, and I wish you all the best."

"Thanks. It's been my pleasure knowing all of you." After returning Anne's hug, he looked at each of them and knew this goodbye wasn't going to be easy. The Baileys were the "salt of the earth," and even though he'd had a rough road for all these months, Luke had been blessed with the friendship he'd found with the Baileys.

"I appreciate all of you and everything you've done for me these past several months," he said. "You'll never know how much it's meant to me. You've been the family I needed all this time."

Luke could see the gloom in everyone's eyes and noticed how tenderly Henry took Norma's hand when her chin began to quiver. It seemed as though their feelings matched the cold rain falling outside.

"Look," Anne said, as if trying to lighten things up, "this isn't going to be goodbye, you know."

"That's true," Norma said, wiping her nose with a hankie. "We won't be living that far apart. We can visit whenever we want, because Lancaster is only about seventy miles from here and not even a two-hour drive."

"Yeah," Luke chimed in. "It's not like I'm goin' across the country. There's a lot to see in Lancaster County, too, so you might enjoy visiting sometime." His eyes stung with tears as he looked at everyone and said, "I have a home that I can share with you now, and boy, does it ever feel good to say that." A lump formed in Luke's throat, and he bowed his head as he tried to find his voice. Looking up, all Luke could do was swallow and whisper, "Thank you, everyone. Thanks a lot."

Philadelphia

The rain had stopped, and the roads were drying off. In less than two hours, Luke would be in Lancaster. Although time seemed to drag, waiting these couple of hours didn't compare to the months he'd been away, trying to remember who he was.

Luke looked down at his jeans, along with the flannel shirt and his red baseball cap. That hat had become part of his daily attire since he'd seen it hanging on the closet door of his room when he'd first arrived in Darby. Luke had gotten used to the English clothing that had been uncomfortable to him at first, but he couldn't wait to get back into his own Plain clothing. He realized that was why these other clothes had never felt quite right.

Luke leaned his head back and closed his eyes. Suddenly, he remembered that he'd been on the bus over a year ago because he'd been heading to Indiana to learn a new trade from his uncle. By now Uncle Amos must have sold the headstone engraving business to someone else.

I'll worry later about how I'm going to support Meredith, he thought. *Right now I just want to get home to her.*

Another thought popped into his head. *Will Meredith be happy to see me? Will she even recognize me in these clothes, with no beard?*

"I'd better pull in here and gas up," Susan said, directing her car into a gas station. "If anyone needs the restroom, now's a good time."

Norma and Luke stepped out of the car, but Henry had his eyes closed and appeared to be asleep.

When Luke was about to leave the restroom a short time later, he stepped up to the sink to wash his hands. He took a quick look in the mirror, and more memories came flooding back. He remembered going to the restroom at the bus station in Philadelphia and seeing a rugged-looking man approach him. The fellow had asked for Luke's clothing and then his wallet. That was the guy who had assaulted him and put him through months of pain and rehab. In those few minutes, Luke's life had changed. The only thing good that had come from the attack was the new friends he had made during his recovery.

I wonder where the attacker is now? Luke thought. *Guess I really don't need to know, now that I'm finally heading home.*

Bird-in-Hand

"What are ya doin' out of bed?" Elam asked Sadie as she stood in front of their bedroom window, staring into the darkness.

"I couldn't sleep," she replied, turning to face him.

"How come?"

"I was remembering the day Luke and Meredith got married. It wasn't that long ago, but it seems like forever."

Elam stepped up to Sadie and slipped his arms around her waist. "It's hard not to look back and remember our youngest child's wedding day.

Especially since this is the eve of Meredith and Jonah's wedding."

"Jah. Levi is a part of our Luke, and I know Meredith and Jonah will make sure Levi knows his father, even though he never had the opportunity to meet him."

"Meredith and Levi are lucky to have Jonah in their lives." Elam paused. "I've seen with my own eyes how Levi looks at Jonah and wants to be held by him."

"You're right. It's hard not to see and hear the love Jonah has for Meredith and Levi." Sadie sighed. "It couldn't have been easy for Jonah to come here and approach me about his feelings for Meredith and Levi some months ago, but I saw right then that Jonah was a sincere, genuine person. How could I fault him for loving Meredith, or deny her and Levi the happiness they deserve?"

Elam gave her a hug. "Luke would be happy to know that his wife and son will be well taken care of. Tomorrow, when we go to the wedding, let's make sure we let them know how happy we are for them, okay?"

Sadie nodded and leaned into her husband's embrace. For the first time in a long while, she felt a true sense of peace—like everything was right in the world.

CHAPTER 11

Ronks

Lying in bed that night, Meredith was having a hard time falling asleep. Was it the anticipation of tomorrow? Was it from all the week's activities? Her whole family was exhausted, but everything was ready for tomorrow.

So why wasn't she asleep? Was she getting cold feet? She didn't remember feeling this way the night before she and Luke got married.

"Stop it," Meredith murmured into the darkness of her room. "I can't compare the way things were with Luke to how they are now; it wouldn't be fair to Jonah."

But could she extract Luke from her heart, even now on the eve of her marriage to Jonah, and go forward? While Meredith wouldn't admit it to Jonah, deep down, she knew she'd never love another man like she had Luke.

After what seemed like hours, she felt her

eyelids growing heavy. *Please Lord*, she silently prayed. *Please let this be right, and help me not to be afraid.*

Afraid of what? she asked herself. She knew the answer but couldn't say it out loud. *You're afraid of making the wrong decision.*

She rolled over and punched her pillow. *I will not let my doubts get in the way of my happiness—or Levi's. Tomorrow morning I will marry Jonah, and that's the end of it.*

Lancaster County, Pennsylvania

The ride to Lancaster went faster than Luke imagined it would. As they got closer, Henry and Norma became more talkative. Listening to them gave Luke a reprieve from practicing what he would say to Meredith. He still didn't know how he would explain everything.

Soon, they were pulling into the driveway. "This is my house," Luke said, opening the car door and getting out. He could hardly believe it, but he was finally home!

"After I speak to Meredith, I'd like you to come in and meet her," Luke said, leaning in the open window of the driver's side.

"Take all the time you need," Henry assured him.

Norma and Susan nodded their agreement.

Luke didn't want to scare Meredith, so he knocked softly on the door. Even so, he expected to hear Fritz bark, like he always did when someone came up to the house.

He was surprised, when a middle-aged English man answered the door.

"Can I help you, sir? Are you lost?" the man asked, looking at Luke with a dubious expression.

"Uh, no, I don't think so. This is my home."

The Englisher shook his head. "My wife and I have been renting this place for a couple of months, so you must have the wrong house."

Luke was completely baffled. Why would Meredith rent out their house, and where was she now? Something wasn't right. Maybe he did have the wrong house. He quickly thanked the man and headed back to Susan's car.

"My memory must not be as clear as I thought it was," he said, opening the car door. "I've gotta be at the wrong house."

"When we pulled in, you said this was your home," Susan said.

"It's the middle of the night," Norma interjected. "Luke, maybe you mistook the place for your own." She motioned to the house. "We saw you talking to a man. What'd he say?"

"Said he and his wife are renting the place."

"Now what? Where do we go from here?" Susan questioned.

With the dome light on in the car, Luke could

see how tired she looked.

"Let's head up the road a ways," he said, getting back into the car. "My folks don't live too far from here. At least, I'm pretty sure this is the road their place is on."

After they'd driven past a few homes, Luke pointed to a mailbox up ahead. Susan pulled over, and Luke got out. It was hard to see in the dark, but using the flashlight Henry had brought along, he was able to see the name on the mailbox: STOLTZFUS.

It was after midnight, and Luke was anxious to see his folks. He didn't want to scare them, yet by the time he got to the door, he was almost desperate. He needed to see someone from his old life—family, friend, anyone.

Luke removed his ball cap and pounded on the door.

After a few minutes, his dad answered. He looked at Luke as if he were a complete stranger.

"Oh, Dad, it's so good to be home." Luke could hardly hold back from throwing himself into his father's arms. He needed to be held, comforted as if he were a little boy again.

Dad pointed the flashlight he was holding at Luke and said, "Who are you?"

"It's me, Luke." Luke knew his voice had taken on a raspy sound from the injury he'd sustained when he was hit in the throat by the mugger, but he was sure his own father would know it was him.

"You're not Luke. Who are you, and what kind of a trick are you playin' on me? My son is dead."

"I'm not dead, Dad. It's really me   your son Luke. I was beat up real bad at the bus station in Philadelphia, and I didn't know who I was until recently." Luke stood, squeezing the red ball cap in his hands.

Dad took a step closer to Luke, studying his face. "Ach!" he shouted, with a catch in his voice. "You've got turquoise eyes just like my son."

"That's right, Dad. I do have turquoise eyes, and I'm telling the truth. I am Luke Stoltzfus, and I'm very much alive."

Dad's eyes widened as though seeing a ghost. Finally, he reached out and grabbed Luke in a hug.

From behind his father, Luke heard a gasp. Mom stepped onto the porch, threw her arms around Luke, and sobbed. "Praise be to God! Our son has been brought back to us!"

"I can't believe I'm sitting here in my kitchen with my son and husband on one side of me and the wonderful people who took my boy in and nursed him back to health on the other side," Sadie said, dabbing at her tears. "It's a miracle beyond belief." She could hardly pull herself away from touching Luke's arm and making sure this was real. Luke was really sitting beside her.

For the last hour, they had listened as their son told of his ordeal—getting mugged, never making it to Indiana, and being in the hospital all those months with no memory of who he was. Susan, Luke's nurse, explained about the surgeries he'd had and the weeks of rehab in the hospital and as an outpatient.

Sadie quickly realized that Luke had been in good hands, treated as if he were part of the Baileys' family. She and Elam owed them a debt of gratitude for taking such good care of their son.

Then Sadie and Elam explained to Luke what they had endured since he'd left. They said the bus he was supposed to have been on had crashed and that all the bodies were burned in the collision.

Henry remarked that the mugger who'd assaulted Luke at the bus depot may have died on that bus, since he'd taken Luke's clothes and his wallet, which held Luke's bus ticket to Indiana.

Elam described the memorial service for Luke and how everyone in their Amish community had grieved, especially Meredith.

Luke nearly jumped out of his chair. "Meredith thinks I'm dead?"

Sadie nodded. "We all thought that, Luke."

"Oh, no," Luke groaned. "I went to my house to see Meredith and was greeted by an English man who said he and his wife were renting the place. Did Meredith move out after she got the

A Vow for Always

news that I was dead?"

Elam shook his head. "Not right away. She had a hard time financially and has been living with her folks for the last couple of months."

Sadie clasped Elam's arm and mouthed something Luke couldn't understand.

"What is it? What's wrong?" he asked. "Is Meredith all right?"

Sadie swallowed hard. "Do you want to tell him, or should I?" she asked, looking solemnly at Elam.

He shrugged. "Whatever you think's best."

Sadie moistened her lips with the tip of her tongue. "A few hours from now, Meredith plans to be married."

Luke's brows furrowed. "What do you mean, Mom? She's already married—to me."

Sadie drew in a quick breath and started again. "As we said, Luke, Meredith believed you were dead, and she grieved for many months until a man named Jonah Miller came into her life. Now she's—"

"Meredith's planning to marry this man?" Luke shouted.

Elam and Sadie nodded. She glanced over at the Baileys and could see the shocked expressions on their faces.

"Luke, you'd better get over to the Kings' place right away," Dad said. "You've got to tell Meredith you're alive!"

109

CHAPTER 12

$\mathcal{L}$uke couldn't believe it. Meredith, believing him dead, was on the brink of marrying another man and starting a new life with him. Even though it was the wee hours of the morning, he had to get to his wife!

Dad offered to hitch his horse to the buggy and take Luke to the Kings' house, but Susan said she would take Luke, as it would be faster by car.

Luke's mother had insisted the Baileys stay with them for the night, and his dad was quick to agree. So while Norma and Henry were shown to their room, Luke and Susan headed to the Kings' place.

Luke was excited to let Meredith know he was alive, yet he was fearful of her response. *What if Meredith loves Jonah now? What if she loves him more than me?*

When they arrived at Philip and Luann's

place, Susan said, "Luke, there's something I need to say."

"What's that?" he asked, turning to look at her.

"I want you to know that I'm happy for you—happy that you're getting your life back."

Luke was tempted to give Susan a hug but thought better of it. Instead, he touched her arm and said, "Thanks, Susan. You've become a good friend, and that means a lot to me."

She smiled and motioned to the house. "You'd better go now. I'll see you before we head back to Darby."

Luke hesitated a moment, then he opened the car door, raced up to the house, and pounded on the door with all his might. "Wake up! Somebody, please answer the door!"

Was she dreaming, or was it time to get up already? Meredith felt like she'd just fallen asleep.

It couldn't be her wedding day already, could it?

Someone was pounding on the front door. Had there been an accident? Did a neighbor need help? Was there a fire somewhere?

She quickly got up when she heard her parents heading down the stairs. Her brain was still fuzzy from waking out of a deep sleep, but Meredith was alert enough to check on Levi. Oblivious to all the noise, her son was sound asleep under his warm blanket.

Meredith slipped into her robe and looked out the window. She couldn't see any blinking lights or flames in the distance. Fritz was whining and waiting for her in the hallway.

Meredith walked to the head of the stairs and went down quietly, as her parents had done minutes ago. She saw them standing at the doorway, but no one was saying anything.

"Mom. . .Dad," Meredith said. "What is it? Who's at the door?"

Her parents turned to face her with unreadable expressions on their faces. Fritz started barking, his tail wagging.

Meredith looked beyond them. A young man stood on the porch. He looked English, right down to the red ball cap he wore on his head. For a fleeting moment, the image of the guy in the hot air balloon she'd seen several months ago crossed her mind. *Silly to be thinking of him at this moment*, she thought.

"What's going on?" Meredith asked, reaching down to grab Fritz's collar.

The young English man hesitated then stepped in front of her.

She clasped her robe tightly, watching as the man removed his ball cap. His hair was short and very blond. She'd never seen hair that blond before, except on Luke.

"Meredith," he said in a raspy voice, "it's me—your husband, Luke."

The ringing in Meredith's ears and Fritz's frantic barking blocked out all other sounds. She glanced quickly at her parents and then looked back at the young man. All she saw was some guy who didn't look or sound like her husband, proclaiming that he was Luke. Who was this man, and why was he playing such a cruel joke?

Speechless, Meredith looked long and hard at the blond-haired man, and that's when she noticed the color of his eyes. Deep turquoise. Her eyes widened, as realization slowly hit—it truly was her husband, Luke. She tried to fight the dark veil of blackness as it came over her from some far-off place. The last thing Meredith remembered was the sensation of being scooped up and looking into those beautiful eyes she'd thought she'd never see again.

"Merrie, wake up!"

What a wonderful sound! She had to be waking up from a dream. Meredith reached out, following the voice. Although a little different, she was sure now that it was indeed her husband's voice.

Slowly she opened her eyes and gazed into the pool of blue that was looking back at her.

Luke had carried her to the sofa and held her in his lap as she came to from her fainting spell.

"How are you feeling, Merrie?" Luke smiled, running his fingers gently over her face.

Meredith smiled back, knowing this was not a dream. No one but Luke had ever called her Merrie. It was like music to her ears.

She sat up quickly, and the most wonderful, euphoric feeling—something she hadn't felt in what seemed like eons—filled her spirit and bubbled over. "Luke, oh Luke! I thought you were dead." Meredith went into her husband's arms and didn't care if she stayed there forever. It felt wonderful being in Luke's warm embrace; she held him so tightly she could hardly breathe.

"Everything's going to be all right now, Merrie." Luke murmured as he held on just as tight.

Meredith leaned back and held on to his precious face, looking into those brilliant eyes. She thought of Psalm 30:11: "Thou hast turned for me my mourning into dancing: thou hast put off my sackcloth, and girded me with gladness." Yes, God had certainly turned her mourning into gladness today.

"I don't know where to begin," she said softly.

"Neither do I," he whispered against her ear. As Luke held Meredith's hand, he relayed to her all that had transpired: the assault at the bus station; his memory loss, surgeries, and rehabilitation;

and the time spent with the Baileys. Luke also mentioned how the Baileys, all except for Anne, had driven him home all the way from Darby.

Meredith leaned into Luke's hand as he gently cupped her face. "I'd like to meet them."

"You will," he assured her.

Meredith shed tears, hearing what Luke had gone through, but now she had something wonderful she wanted to share with her husband. Something she knew would erase the weeks and months of pain they'd both endured.

Before she could voice the words, Luke lifted her chin so she was looking into his eyes and said, "Meredith, I need to ask your forgiveness for the things I said to you before leaving on my trip."

She sniffed deeply. "I forgive you, but I need to apologize for my part in the disagreements we had, as well."

"No more regrets," he told her. "It's just you and me now, and we have our whole lives before us. We can start over with a clean slate."

"It's not just you and me anymore," Meredith said, feeling so happy she thought she'd burst. "There's someone I'd like you to meet." She reached for Luke's hand. "Come with me to my room."

When they entered Meredith's bedroom, she led Luke over to the crib that held her precious surprise. She watched Luke's expression as he looked from Meredith to the little angel sleeping soundly while sucking his thumb.

"Luke," she whispered, "meet your son, Levi."

Luke drew in a sharp breath. His face broke into a wide smile. "We have a little *bu?*"

She nodded. "I suspected I was pregnant before you left on the bus, but I didn't want to tell you until I knew for sure. I was planning to give you the news as soon as you returned from Indiana." Her voice faltered. "Of course that never happened."

"Meredith, I'm so sorry," he apologized, slipping his little finger into Levi's grasp.

Levi's small hand held tight to his daddy's finger, as if feeling the love pass from father to son. It was a beautiful moment, and among many she would never forget.

She took Luke's hand, and they sat on the bed, watching Levi's even breathing, while Meredith explained everything to Luke about the birth of their son. Then, as if everything else had disappeared, Meredith remembered that her wedding to Jonah was supposed to happen in a few hours. Now she knew why those voices of doubt had kept troubling her about marrying Jonah. She realized what she felt for him had more to do with how good he was to her son and the fact that Levi needed a father. Even though Meredith knew it would hurt Jonah, she had to tell him right away. Jonah was kind and sincere and had been a good friend. She hated the thought that she was about to bring him pain.

As the sun rose, Meredith explained the situation to Luke, and when she said she needed to tell Jonah right away, Luke nodded with understanding and said, "I'll go with you, Merrie."

Bird-in-Hand

Jonah had been awake since early that morning, unable to sleep. Finally his wedding day had arrived. He looked outside and whistled, seeing a beautiful day unfolding. The rain had moved out, and the fog was lifting, forming white wispy clouds against the bluest of skies. It looked almost too perfect for words. Today he would marry his true love, and he could hardly wait.

Jonah took a seat at the kitchen table. He was the only one up, but his parents would be coming down shortly; he'd heard them stirring in their room upstairs.

Herbie started barking, and Jonah glanced out the window, seeing a horse and buggy pull up. When he opened the front door, he was surprised to see Meredith.

"Come in." He smiled at his soon-to-be wife. "I didn't expect to see you this early."

"Jonah," she said, biting her lip, "I need to speak with you about something."

Jonah stiffened. Something was wrong. He could see the wary expression on Meredith's face. "What's going on?" he asked. "Why are you here so early?"

She motioned to the kitchen table. "Please, sit down."

Jonah did as she asked, and she took a seat across from him.

"I don't know any other way to say this, but Luke isn't dead," she said, speaking softly and slowly. "He came to my folks' house late last night." Meredith paused. "Jonah, my husband has returned to me."

Jonah didn't believe her. "Are you making this up because you've changed your mind and don't want to marry me?" he asked. He had always sensed a bit of reluctance in Meredith, even when he thought they had everything worked out.

Meredith shook her head forcibly. "It's the truth, and I feel bad telling you this way. The last thing I'd ever want to do is hurt you, Jonah."

"How can Luke be alive? I mean, the sheriff told you that Luke had been killed when the bus was hit by a tanker full of gas."

She nodded. "It's true. The bus exploded. But Luke wasn't on it."

"He wasn't?"

"No. Some man wanting Luke's money beat him up at the bus station in Philadelphia. When Luke regained consciousness, he didn't know who he was. He was injured quite badly and spent some time in the hospital. After that, some really nice folks took him in, and that's where he's been all this time. It's just been recently that Luke's memory returned."

"If this is all true—"

"It is, Jonah. Luke's outside in my buggy right now."

Jonah went over to the window. He could see the silhouette of a man sitting in the buggy, holding the reins. "He doesn't look like an Amish man," Jonah protested. "He's not wearing Amish clothes, and where's his beard?"

"It's a long story," Meredith said, "but my husband has returned, and we can't be married." She blinked, as though fighting back tears. Not wishing to make things any harder for her, Jonah decided to deal with her news the best way he could, although inside his heart was breaking. Jonah wanted so badly to be Meredith's husband. Obviously, that was not meant to be.

Luke waited nervously in the buggy, wondering how things were going with Meredith and the man she was supposed to marry—a man Luke had never met. Luke had watched as Meredith knocked on the door. She'd turned back and waved reassuringly to him.

Out of the blue, another image entered Luke's mind. On the day he'd gone up in the hot air balloon, he'd noticed a woman walking toward the parking area. For a moment she had turned, watching him, and then she'd waved back as the balloon he was in went higher and higher. Luke would have to share that story with Meredith later on. It was wonderful, knowing they had the rest of their lives ahead of them to plan, share, and grow old together. God had given them both a second chance.

But how would Jonah take the news? Would he be upset? Would he wish Luke really were dead?

The front door opened, and Meredith came out of the house with a man walking behind her. The guy looked nice enough, although even from this distance, Luke could see a hint of sadness in his eyes.

When Meredith and Jonah approached the buggy, Luke got out and tied the reins to the hitching post. It was an odd situation, and Luke struggled for something to say.

Jonah stared back at him with a startled expression.

Luke, unsure of what to do, extended his hand to the man. They shook hands, but Jonah continued to stare at him strangely.

Meredith glanced at Luke, and after a few more awkward moments, she introduced them to each other. Once the introductions had been made, she turned to Jonah and said, "Are you okay?"

Jonah glanced at Meredith and then back at Luke. His voice cracked as he stammered, "It—it's you! You're the one. I'd remember those turquoise eyes anywhere."

Luke, feeling quite confused, asked what Jonah meant.

"A long time ago when I was a boy, I nearly drowned."

"Jah," Meredith said. "I remember you told me what a lasting impression that boy had made on your life."

Jonah nodded. "Being pulled to the surface of that deep cold pond, I saw these kind, caring eyes of such a different color. They looked into my own eyes and gave me silent encouragement to hang on. I never thought I'd come face-to-face with that boy again, and yet, here you are."

Luke rubbed the bridge of his nose as he thought hard and long. When he was thirteen, he'd spent a week with his aunt and uncle in Ohio. He'd gone fishing one day with his cousin and had saved a boy from drowning. He hadn't thought much of it because he'd always been a good swimmer and his parents had taught him to offer help whenever he could.

Jonah pointed to Luke and said, "You are that boy, aren't you?"

"I guess so." Suddenly, Luke realized he and Jonah had a special connection—what could be a lasting bond.

Jonah clasped Luke's shoulder. "You have a very special wife, and I know you two will be happy together for the rest of your lives. I'd be lying if I didn't say that I love her, but I've always known she's never loved me the way she does you."

Tears welled in Meredith's eyes, and Luke felt moisture on his cheeks, too. No wonder Meredith had agreed to marry Jonah. He truly was a fine man.

Luke shook Jonah's hand once more, and then as he and Meredith climbed into their buggy, he thanked God for bringing them together again.

Luke realized that if he hadn't been mugged and had continued on the bus ride to his uncle's, he wouldn't be alive today. Maybe that was God's way of saying thank you for saving a young boy's life a long time ago. Some things were hard to figure out, but no matter what the future held, he and Meredith would make it through, because they had each other and God.

EPILOGUE

Six months later

Come sit with me as I read the letter we just received from Jonah," Meredith said, motioning Luke to the sofa.

Holding Levi, Luke settled down beside her, anxious to hear what Jonah had to say. Just a few weeks after Luke had returned home, Jonah had moved to Illinois, where his twin sister and her family lived. He'd started a buggy-making business and was doing quite well. It would have been difficult for Jonah to stay in Lancaster County, where he'd be reminded of his love for Meredith every time he saw her.

"Jonah's found a girlfriend," Meredith said, smiling at Luke. "Or at least he's found someone he's interested in. He says he's not sure if she returns his feelings, but he's going to pursue her and see what develops."

"That's great." *A new life for Jonah, and a second chance for me*, Luke thought. "Isn't it amazing how the difficulties we experienced for more than a year turned into blessings for everyone involved? I not only have my life back with my beautiful wife"—he smiled at her—"but I also have an adorable son and a future full of plans and dreams. And let's not forget the Baileys," he added.

"Jah, that's right." Meredith rested her head on Luke's shoulder.

The Bailey family had become special to everyone in Meredith and Luke's families. Several visits had occurred over the summer, and Luke was happy to learn that Susan had someone special in her life whom she'd met at church.

And Luke didn't have to worry about how to provide for his family. Fortunately, Uncle Amos had not sold his business when Luke was presumed dead, so Luke had taken it over just as they had originally planned. But true happiness didn't come from financial security, Luke had learned. It came from being with those he loved and letting others see God's love through his actions.

ABOUT THE AUTHOR

New York Times bestselling author Wanda E. Brunstetter became fascinated with the Amish way of life when she first visited her husband's Mennonite relatives living in Pennsylvania. Wanda and her husband, Richard, live in Washington State but take every opportunity to visit Amish settlements throughout the States, where they have several Amish friends. Wanda and her husband have two grown children and six grandchildren. In her spare time, Wanda enjoys photography, ventriloquism, gardening, beachcombing, and having fun with her family.

Visit Wanda's website at www.wandabrunstetter.com.

OTHER BOOKS BY WANDA E. BRUNSTETTER

Adult Fiction

KENTUCKY BROTHERS SERIES
The Journey
The Healing
The Struggle

BRIDES OF LEHIGH CANAL SERIES
Kelly's Chance
Betsy's Return
Sarah's Choice

INDIANA COUSINS SERIES
A Cousin's Promise
A Cousin's Prayer
A Cousin's Challenge

SISTERS OF HOLMES COUNTY SERIES
A Sister's Secret
A Sister's Test
A Sister's Hope

BRIDES OF WEBSTER COUNTY SERIES
Going Home
Dear to Me
On Her Own
Allison's Journey

DAUGHTERS OF LANCASTER COUNTY SERIES
The Storekeeper's Daughter
The Quilter's Daughter
The Bishop's Daughter